STRIP TEASE

ERIN MCCARTHY

Cover art by Hang Le

Connect with Erin:

Twitter

Facebook

Goodreads

www.erinmccarthy.net

ONE

"SHOULD I take my shirt off first or my pants?" Brandon Blackwell asked Lilly, hands on the zipper of his pants. He'd always been a free-the-beast-first kind of guy.

"Don't you think we're beyond taking the pants off?" Lilly asked. "Do we really need to do that?"

That made him grin. "Don't cramp my style, Lil."

His old friend rolled her eyes. "What do you guys think?" she asked his other childhood buddies, Rick, Axl, and Jesse. "This is year three for this charity strip event. Isn't it time to keep the pants on?"

"I'm cool with that," Rick said. "I'm married now. Sloane's been a good sport but I'm sure she'd appreciate it if I kept my pants on."

"Same," Axl said. "This is the first time I'm doing this with a girlfriend and I want to be sensitive to Leighton's feelings."

Brandon groaned and turned to Sullivan, the owner of Tap That bar, who was leaning against the back of the bar, arms crossed over his chest. Sullivan was looking smug that he wasn't participating in the dancing Lilly loved to choreograph.

"Get me a whiskey, bro," Brandon said. "I'm thirsty from arguing with all our pussy-whipped friends."

Sullivan grinned. "If you want to start a tab I need a credit card."

"Oh, fuck off. I'm only here because of you." These guys had been his friends since grade school and they loved to give each other shit. Sullivan wouldn't charge him any more than Brandon would refuse to show up for this event. Even though Sullivan would never get gushy about any of this they all knew he appreciated they were doing this in his late wife's honor.

Sometimes, it was hard to believe Kendra had been gone three years. At least Sullivan seemed to be handling it better. He'd laid off the drinking and had mellowed out a bit.

"Doesn't mean I want to see your junk on my stage," Sullivan said. He turned and reached for a bottle of whiskey.

"That makes you the only one."

"Honestly, I can say I don't," Lilly said with a smirk. "I've seen far too much of the four of you already."

"You love it and you know it." Brandon took the whiskey from Sullivan and tossed it back. If he had to guess, Sullivan was the only one Lilly *would* want to see in his underwear and his friend was being too stubborn to notice.

Lilly shook her head. "Negative."

"Back me up, Lambert," Brandon said to Jesse, who was single and a pro hockey player. "The ladies love it when we get down to the bare essentials."

"I'm on your side," Jesse said. "You and me take it down to shorts, these other guys who have women to answer to can keep it on. More applause for us. Works for me."

"Fine," Lilly said. "I agree that the women love it. I concede that point. I may have to do some line shifting. Like we start Axl and Rick out in the front and then you and Jesse burst out between them."

"And now you ruined it, Lil. Bursting?" Brandon grimaced. "Let's just run through this, okay? I have to get back to Chicago before Monday."

"It's Saturday at three in the afternoon. Chill," she commanded.

"The way we're going we'll be here all night," Axl said. "Just tell me when to pivot and I'm on it." He pulled his phone out and glanced at it and grinned.

"What are you looking at? If it's funny, share it." Brandon was almost positive it would be from Axl's girl, but that made giving Axl crap even more fun. He was happy for Rick and Axl. He really was. Didn't mean he wanted to join them in the couples' crowd.

"It's none of your business," Axl said. "Just something from Leighton."

For half a second, seeing his buddy with that smile on his face, looking lovesick as fuck, Brandon envied him.

Then the split second passed.

He wasn't even thirty yet and he was in no hurry to settle down.

His career was going gangbusters. He was independently wealthy, with a growing portfolio of business holdings and an expensive condo in Lincoln Park in Chicago. He had a closetful of Armani and Hugo Boss suits and a Mercedes.

His partying had grown up into whiskey tastings and weekends in Turks and Caicos but he still went hard after a good time.

Which meant he was also still enjoying the ladies. Plural being the key word. *Ladies.* Not just one.

Life was pretty damn perfect and he had no intention of changing a thing.

"Give me a beat, Lil," he said, unbuttoning his shirt. "I need to beat out Jesse for Beaver Bend's most eligible bachelor."

"I'm a pro hockey player," Jesse said. "I win."

"I make more money and I dance better."

Bring on the ladies.

"PROFESSIONAL HOCKEY PLAYER Jesse Lambert in annual strip show." Grace Martinez read the headline out loud as she stared at her phone screen. "I wouldn't hate to see that."

Anything that had to do with hockey, her favorite sport of all time, she would probably click on. But add to that hot men stripping, at least one of whom was a pro player? She was so in. It was the only action she was going to get these days. She couldn't even remember the last time she'd had sex but it wasn't this year, she knew that for sure.

Being a single mom of an eight-year-old had a lot of challenges, and dating was one of them. So, rolling her chair back a little away from her at-home work station, she propped her legs up on the desk and turned her phone to make the video bigger.

A blonde newscaster was speaking. "Jesse Lambert will be back in Northern Minnesota next week for the third annual Tap That Charity Strip Show. He will be dancing to raise money for breast cancer awareness after his childhood friend lost his wife three years ago."

"That's nice," Grace said out loud again. She talked out loud more than she liked to admit. It was an occupational hazard of working at home and having spent the bulk of her twenties alone with her daughter. Kids weren't known for their intellectual discourse.

She wondered what the newscaster meant by Northern Minnesota. If Grace could get her brother to take Fallon for a few hours, she could have her first girls' night out in forever if the drive wasn't too far. It was for charity so that meant zero guilt. The idea of watching a bunch of men gyrate wasn't normally her go-to entertainment but she really dug Jesse Lambert as a player. Besides, she hadn't gone out at night in six months, unless taking Fallon to Girl Scout meetings qualified as going out.

As she plotted, Grace watched the footage from the year before of four guys dancing. Jesse Lambert was no Channing Tatum. He had zero rhythm. She'd seen a newborn giraffe minutes after birth with more understanding of what his legs could do than Jesse. Which was insane given the man spent half his life on skates on ice with a large stick in his hand.

Amused, Grace reached for her coffee, her mug stating "Every day I'm Hustlin'," and took a sip. Damn, it was cold. She frowned at her mug and set it back down, eyes off her phone momentarily. When her gaze flickered back to the screen, she nearly dropped the phone, her heart rate shooting up and her palms instantly going clammy.

"Oh my God," she murmured, feet falling back to the floor as she tried to pause the video. She couldn't get it to stop and she frantically touched her screen, afraid that face was going to go away.

Finally, she got it to pause, and right there, on the screen, in mid hip thrust, a smirk of epic proportions on his face, was the guy she'd met here in Minneapolis nine years ago when she'd been a naïve college student, more bravado than common sense. It had been his twenty-first birthday and he'd danced with her at a bar, fed her many lines of bullshit, including a fake name and fake number, then had sex with her.

He'd been gone from her dorm room before she'd woken up and it had taken her a day or two to realize he'd lied about who he was and she was never going to hear from him again. It had taken another six weeks to realize she was pregnant.

And now, here he was on her phone. *Thank you, technology.*

Her hands were trembling as she let the video play to the

end, watching her sperm donor perform his way through a dance routine in a very expensive-looking suit. He looked more built, more chiseled than she remembered. His youthful face had become more manly, though he moved with the same easy confidence she remembered from that night. She had been naked before she could even think about it. That's how damn charming and bold he had been.

The memory of his features had faded over the years, especially given that she'd been drinking Jager bombs that night and everything was a little bright and fuzzy on reflection. But now she saw that Fallon had his eyes, his nose, and his dimples. How completely and utterly bizarre to be looking at a total stranger whose DNA made up half of her amazing and beautiful little girl.

Okay, so not a *total* stranger.

Grace remembered those hot, deep kisses on the patio behind the bar, snow silently falling on them. He'd pulled up her hood on her coat to keep the snow from dampening her hair, and he'd cupped her cheeks with ease, kissing her until her head had spun and she found herself pressing her hips against his, wanting to feel his cock, her inner thighs hot. She'd been excited, eager, and minutes later back in her room, he'd given her an orgasm.

Then she'd passed out from drinking and sex, and woken up to find him gone and a busted purple party condom still lying on her nightstand, mostly empty. Sitting up, head pounding, she realized unlike the condom, her vagina was not empty. He'd left her with the gift that kept on giving, running down her leg.

All these years later, she didn't regret a damn thing. She wouldn't trade Fallon for anything in the world. Her daughter had forced her to grow up, had given her a focus, and made her realize that she could love someone to the very marrow of her bones. Fallon was, without question, the best thing to ever happen to her.

That didn't mean she wasn't going to show up at that charity strip event and call Sperm Donor out. You want to play, you should have to pay. She wanted to look him in the eye and let him know, for Fallon's sake, that he had a daughter. What he chose to do after that was on him and fine with her, but she owed her daughter this.

Besides, she personally wanted the opportunity to point out he'd been an ass. Just once, then she would drop it.

Copying the link, she sent the video to her best friend from college, Siobhan.

Recognize the guy in the suit?

Siobhan texted back right away.

No, why? Who is that? He's hot.

Jeff Spicoli. Nine years ago. Lucky's bar.

Grace still couldn't believe she'd been stupid enough to fall for that fake name. Jeff Spicoli. Geez. But she'd never seen Fast Times at Ridgemont High because the movie was way before her time, and she wasn't a guy. She didn't think stoner jokes or bro movies were funny. Vampires were more her thing. It wasn't until she couldn't find Sperm Donor online anywhere later that day that she had told Siobhan what his alleged full name was. Her best friend had enlightened her she'd been played. Big-time.

Siobhan's face popped up on her screen.

Grace answered her call without a greeting. "Can you freaking believe it? Nine years. Nine damn years and there he is. Strutting his stuff."

"Holy fucking shit," was Siobhan's opinion. "I mean, I thought he looked familiar at first but I couldn't place it. Then as soon as you said it, boom, the memory came flooding back. It's *totally* him. Same dance moves."

"Right?" Grace rubbed her temple and turned to her desktop computer to pull that video up again. She felt the need to compulsively view it over and over. "He's stripping for charity. Why am I not surprised?"

"I mean, that's nice, I guess. It's charity. But still arrogant as fuck. Do you know anything about him? What the hell is his real name?"

"No idea. But I will find out. Give me thirty minutes."

"Are you going to try to talk to him?" Siobhan asked. "I support you either way, for the record. Personally, I would like to give his nuts a good squeeze and tell him what a tool he is, but I know that's not exactly your style."

Grace had every intention of giving him a piece of her mind. Because what still pissed her off all these years later was the complete lack of honesty. Even as a naïve eighteen-year-old freshman she had known it was just a hookup. She might have stalked him online but she would not have expected a relationship or gone psycho. She'd fallen into bed with him fueled on freedom from her grandmother's upbringing, alcohol, and the heady cocktail of lust and longing.

Jeff Spicoli.

Please.

"Oh, trust me I am going to confront him. It's the right thing for Fallon. You know she asks like once a week who her father is and my answer is frustrating for her."

It was awkward as hell to explain over and over to her daughter that she did not know her father's real name.

"I've always felt partly responsible. I encouraged you to dance with him that night."

That made Grace laugh as she watched the video again on mute, studying his face. She almost felt bad that she was about to rock his world. Or maybe it wouldn't matter to him. Maybe he wouldn't give two shits. Maybe he would shrug it off. She did want to know if he was married or not. It was certainly possible. He'd be almost thirty by now. It would be far easier to break her news to him if he wasn't. Less complicated.

"You are not responsible, Siobhan. I was giddy from being out from under my grandmother's strict rules and I had hormones raging. Guys aren't the only ones who can claim hormones made them do it. I saw him and I had a serious case of lust."

"Does this mean we're road tripping north this weekend? I need to cancel my current plans."

"You really want to go with me?" Grace would go either way, but she would love Siobhan as her wingman. For the emotional support and because it felt right. Full circle. Siobhan was the only friend who had been there that night and the one who had hugged her when she had cried over that pregnancy test.

Siobhan snorted. "Oh, I wouldn't miss this shit for the world. A town called Beaver Bend. Jeff Spicoli run to ground. Strippers. I'm already packing."

"Awesome. Let me figure out all the details of this charity show and find us a hotel and I will call you back later."

"Roger that."

It took ten minutes to find his real name. She found an article in the local Beaver Bend paper outlining all the guys in the show and their real-life occupations. By process of elimination based on what they were wearing for the strip show, he had to be Brandon Blackwell.

"Brandon Blackwell." Grace turned the name around in her head. "Brandon." He looked like a Brandon. Middle class frat boy. That's what he had been then.

Now he appeared to have life by the tail. It only took another ten minutes to find out he owned multiple companies, appeared to live in a condo with a view of Lake Michigan, and traveled like a rock star.

She kind of hated him.

Every other picture of him on social media was with a cocktail in one hand, a hot girl in the other.

She'd been wrong. It would be better if he were married. At least then she would respect that he was capable of commitment. He didn't even appear to have a dog or a cat. Just lots of money and pretty girls.

She wondered what stupid alias he gave them.

Maybe he'd graduated to Christian Grey.

It was a four-hour drive to Beaver Bend. She called her brother, Juan, her only family now that her grandmother has passed away. "Hey, can Fallon spend the night with you and Mina on Friday?" Her brother was still a newlywed but she didn't think he would mind too much.

"Sure, why? Got a hot date?"

She stared at her computer screen. Brandon Blackwell stared back at her on a balcony in South Beach, sunglasses on, shirtless. "Nope. I found Fallon's father. I'm going to talk to him."

"You *what*?" Her brother instantly sounded more alert. "I'm going with you. Fallon can stay with Mina."

"No. Hell no. You'll kick his ass and that's not what this is about. Siobhan is going with me."

"I want to go."

"Forget it." Juan would start the conversation with his fist and that would get them nowhere but arrested.

"Well, who the hell is he?"

"His name is Brandon."

"So what does he look like?"

Annoyed, she rolled her eyes even though he couldn't see her. "Juan, like an older version of how he looked at twenty-one.

I had sex with him, remember? Don't act like I got pregnant unconscious. He didn't do anything wrong. It was one hundred percent consensual." On that she was one hundred percent certain. She remembered those hot kisses and that orgasm more than she had remembered his face.

Her brother grumbled. She knew that he hated to think she had a sex life. Or that she had once upon a time. She didn't currently.

"So, what does he do for a living? Is he a loser?"

"Not at all. He's not a felon either. He's a successful businessman living in Chicago." Which seemed ironic, given she and Juan had grown up in Chicago.

"I want to be angry, but I guess I can't be angry about that."

"That's not exactly how I feel." She clicked on Brandon's photo and made it bigger. Damn it, he was good-looking. "I seem to be getting angrier by the minute."

If he had a passel of illegitimate children flung all over the Great Lakes region, she wasn't sure what she would do with that.

"Cool it, Rocky. If he needs a pop in the mouth, let Siobhan do it."

That made her laugh. "No one is popping anyone. I'm a mother. I don't advocate violence."

All she wanted to do was talk.

She played the stripping video again.

Yep. Just talk.

Grace fanned herself and shoved all thoughts of sex aside.

For the most part.

TWO

PANTIES HIT Brandon on the arm as he ripped off his shirt. He grinned at the screaming crowd. Panties being tossed at them was new this year. The event was getting wilder by the minute. Rick and Axl had retreated to the back of the stage, and truthfully Brandon could see why. Even the most understanding wife or girlfriend wouldn't be thrilled at her partner being nailed with lingerie.

On the other hand, as a very single guy, he thought it was hilarious.

The music playing was some deep grinding R&B. Classic stripper music. Brandon tossed his shirt into the crowd. A short redhead caught it, leaping with impressive dexterity to beat out her taller competitors. She let out a scream of triumph and Brandon found himself impressed with her tenacity and enthusiasm. He was a guy who liked to sample all shapes and sizes and he instantly imagined diving into all those beautiful curves. She looked like a fun girl.

Then he accidentally locked eyes with a leggy brunette right next to the redhead.

The brunette didn't look impressed with his moves.

In fact, she was glaring at him.

Then she shocked him by ripping the shirt right out of her friend's hand, bunching it up into a ball, and tossing it back at him. He didn't react fast enough and it hit him in the face.

Next to him, Jesse laughed.

Brandon dropped the shirt and raised his eyebrows in question at the brunette. She rolled her eyes and crossed her arms over her chest.

She was a beautiful woman. A cranky, beautiful woman.

Maybe she was married and thought strip shows were stupid.

Maybe she had a headache.

Brandon shifted to the left, smiling and pointing out to the crowd in that direction, a little thrown off by the brunette.

But when he turned back to the center again, she was still glaring at him. The redhead was dancing and clapping her hands. The brunette was standing legs slightly apart, stock-still. She had long wavy hair that was a deep caramel color, and very long lashes. Her eyes looked to be amber, and she had full lips, turned down in a frown. He wondered if he'd blown her off in high school or something. She looked familiar but he couldn't place her. They were a dozen years out from school. Maybe she'd been a Plain Jane back in the day and he had been dismissive of her.

It was possible. He hadn't been a dick to girls in school but he'd also been oblivious to girls who weren't smoking hot. He'd had a one-track mind back then.

He didn't think that was it, though. He felt like she would never have been plain, and he felt... something. A tug. Like he knew her. Intimately.

Whatever it was, he wished she would stop giving him the evil eye. It was throwing off his rhythm.

"Guys, it's that time," Lilly said over the mic.

It was a welcome interruption. "What time is that?" he asked, following the cue they'd established in rehearsal.

"Time to pull a lucky lady from our group of donors to dance with you!"

Lilly did a great job of engaging the crowd and all the women screamed at her words. Brandon knew who he was going to bring up on stage. The redhead.

Rick picked out Sloane, of course, and they started dancing, both laughing. Axl brought up his girlfriend, Leighton, and they did a slow dance that had nothing whatsoever to do with the music playing. But they were gazing into each other's eyes in adoration and Brandon thought he'd need a fucking insulin shot after watching something that damn sweet. Jesse grabbed a woman who was wearing his hockey jersey. Her cheeks turned red and her hands shook, she was so excited.

Brandon walked straight up to the redhead. He held out his hand. "Care to dance?"

Her hand was already coming out to take his when the brunette knocked it away. "Siobhan, you are not dancing with him!"

"Shit, sorry, I lost my head for a second," the redhead said, making a face. "You know me. Music, booze, bare chests. I have zero self-control." She gave him an apologetic shrug.

Annoyed by the cockblock, he turned to the brunette. "And why can't she dance with me? I promise to behave myself."

She snorted. She actually snorted. "Just pick someone else."

Oh, she fucking walked right into that one. "Okay. I pick you."

Her jaw dropped. "What? No!"

But he had already had his hand wrapped around hers and he tugged her a little. "I don't bite."

"I'm not dancing with you!"

"It's either you or her," he said, gesturing to her friend. "I will stand here and make a scene." He gave her an easy smile.

"Just let me dance with him, Grace," the redhead, Siobhan, said.

Grace. Interesting name for a woman who looked like she could disembowel him with her bare hands, given half a chance. The name didn't trigger any memories, which was driving him insane. He had to know who she was.

"I'd love to dance with you, Siobhan."

"No way in hell," Grace replied. "Just stop flirting with my friend," she told him.

"Jealous?" he asked with a smirk.

Her eyebrows shot up and she suddenly looked flustered. "Fine. One song. I'll dance with you."

He hadn't expected her to give in so easily. "Fabulous." He squeezed her hand and pulled her toward him.

She looked up at him under those insanely long eyelashes, an emotion he didn't understand in her eyes.

Brandon paused, puzzled. *Did* he know her? Something about that expression... it was gone before he could figure the feeling out.

When he reached the stage and stepped up onto it, he helped Grace join him, but then she immediately pulled her hand out of his. She danced to the music, but she didn't look at him. Her movements were fluid, graceful. She was wearing denim shorts and a plain black V-neck T-shirt with red Converse. She hadn't dressed to be seductive but she had long legs and a waist that dipped in and made him want to grip her with both hands and pull her body against his.

He resisted the urge because most likely she would slap him.

The music changed then, to a slow baby-making song.

Grace shifted like she was going to bolt from the stage, but he stopped her, and before she could resist, he pulled her in for a slow dance.

"Let me go," she said, her voice calm, belying the anger in her eyes.

"Have we met before?" he asked, because it was clear she had some sort of personal feeling toward him, and not a good one.

He liked to think that he remembered all the women he had sex with, especially in his hometown, so he was confused as to why he couldn't place her if he had. Yes, he'd been with a lot of women. But he really did remember all of them. Names, places. Grace wasn't triggering any memories, and he was convinced it was because it was out of context. He must know her from somewhere else. Not here.

Grace surprised him by giving him a short laugh. But then she draped her arms over his shoulders and settled into the dance, like she'd gained the upper hand. "Yes, we have met. In Minneapolis. Nine years ago."

Nine years ago? Jesus. He fished around for what the fuck he might have been doing in Minneapolis nine years ago. He hadn't spent much time there, going to college in Chicago. The only reason he would go to Minneapolis was to meet up with his childhood buddies from time to time. Like for his twenty-first birthday. That had been a wild night. A string of bars and free shots and then a leggy brunette's dorm room...

Oh, fuck, and there it was. He knew exactly who she was.

He had met her on the dance floor at a bar, already drunk and well on his way to wasted. He had thought she was pretty and tall and funny. She had laughed at all his dumb jokes, and tossed much more intelligent ones back at him.

"My twenty-first birthday," he said. "We went back to your dorm."

She nodded. "Wow, I'm impressed. I thought I would have to feed you more prompts than that."

He pulled her a little closer to him, but she held herself away, like she was afraid to have her body touch his. He remembered having fun that night, so why the hell was she mad at him all these years later? Sure, he'd left without saying anything other than his number scrawled on a piece of paper but that was before the days of Uber and Lyft and Axl had been banging on the door telling him they were leaving without him if he didn't get his ass out of bed.

"I have a good memory when it comes to beautiful women," he said. "It's good to see you again, Grace. Wow, crazy to run into you here in Beaver Bend after all these years." He gave her a grin. "Thanks for making my twenty-first birthday extra fun."

"No problem, *Jeff*," she said, rolling her eyes.

Jeff? "Excuse me?"

"Jeff Spicoli. That's the fake name you gave me. To go with the fake number you left on my nightstand when you left without saying goodbye."

Fuck. He had done that. Brandon shifted so that they were more toward the back of the stage, away from prying eyes. "Sorry, I have no excuse for the name thing other than my friends and I had all decided on movie names when we pregamed before hitting the bars. It was stupid. But I did give you the right number." He wouldn't have bothered to give a number at all if he didn't want to hear from her. Giving a fake number was a dick move and not something he'd ever done.

"No, you didn't. I tried that number a few weeks later and it belonged to a girl named Hannah who didn't appreciate my texts."

"I was still drunk when I left. Maybe my handwriting sucked. My friends were leaving, I had to go in a hurry." He leaned in closer to her, and whispered in her ear. "Trust me, I would have loved to have seen you again." That was the truth.

They'd had a great connection in spite of him being loaded and ridiculous. Nothing between them had been bumbling or awkward. The sex had been amazing, the chemistry real. He would have seen her again sober. He'd been disappointed when she hadn't texted him.

"I wasn't texting you for a booty call or a date. I was trying to reach you to tell you I was pregnant."

Brandon jolted. Her words hit him like an electrical charge. "*What*? Are you fucking kidding me?" Pregnant? She'd gotten *pregnant*?

Grace nodded. "Yes. Apparently purple party condoms aren't reliable. It broke and I got pregnant."

His heart was pounding and his palms were suddenly damp with sweat. "What... what did you do?" What the fuck was she actually telling him?

Her eyes softened then. "I had the baby, Brandon. She's eight years old now and she'd pretty amazing, I have to say."

For a split second, he thought he was going to go down like a stone. The room went black and the music seemed to be pulsing from inside his body and flinging outward. The bass pounded in time with his heart. He had a kid. Holy shit, he had a kid and he had known nothing about it.

The song ended and he stared at Grace, speechless.

She pulled away from him.

Then she bolted, pushing her way through the crowd, heading for the exit.

Brandon spared a glance at Lilly and told her, "I have to go."

The room felt hot and loud and he was in shock. He followed Grace, maneuvering his way as quickly as possible through the women grinning at him and trying to talk to him. He ignored everyone, rocked to his core. He had to get to Grace.

Bursting out through the front door of the bar, he found her leaning against the brick wall, her hands over her face. She was standing under the fluorescent Tap That sign and he swore under his breath. He had tapped that and he'd gotten her pregnant.

Fuckity fuck and fuck.

He approached her, not sure what in the hell to say, but knowing he had to untie his tongue and say something. He owed Grace the mother of all apologies.

And he had a kid he now desperately wanted to know everything about.

"GRACE."

Grace wiped her tears away and took a deep breath. She had not meant to tell Brandon on the dance floor. But she'd waited nine years for this moment and it had just come flying out of her mouth. Steeling herself, she peeled her body off the wall she had been using to prevent from dropping to her knees, and turned to see Brandon standing there shirtless, under the bright lights, looking shell-shocked and stricken.

"I'm sorry, Grace," he said. "I'm so sorry. I... I don't know what to say. I wish I had known. And I'm sorry I used a purple condom. And that I was an asshole who gave you a stupid fake name. I'm sorry."

Grace wiped her hands on the front of her shorts. She had wondered many times over the years what her sperm donor would say if she ever had the opportunity to tell him the truth. Most of the time, she concluded that he would probably shrug and say it had been an accident. That he might try to charm her in some way or blow it off. But Brandon looked genuinely contrite and horrified and everything he should. She actually believed in his apology.

"Thank you for saying that," she said. "And I'm sorry for blurting it out like that. I didn't mean to do that. It's just it's been inside me so long and when I figured out who you were three days ago, I've just been nonstop thinking about this." She took a deep breath. "I don't expect anything, you know. That's not what this is about. I just thought you had a right to know now that I know your real name."

She was still getting used to his real name. He'd been Jeff even after she'd known it was a fake name. And sperm donor. But even though she'd known for three days his name was Brandon, her head was still adjusting.

His hands were on his hips and he dropped them, swallowing visibly. Brandon had short dark hair, a strong jaw, and blue eyes that had made her weak in the knees. She suddenly felt like she might cry and he noticed.

He moved toward her, opening his arms. "Come here."

Grace went into his hug without hesitation because damn it, it was a relief to get a secret she had never intended to be a secret off of her chest. She leaned against his shoulder and sighed, tears welling in her eyes.

"You must be an amazing woman," he murmured, rubbing the small of her back gently. "And thank you for raising our daughter by yourself."

Our daughter. Oh, God. Until this very moment, Fallon had been hers. Hers alone. Grace pulled back to look at him, unsure what to say.

Fortunately, she was saved by Siobhan coming out of the bar. "Grace, are you okay?"

"I'm fine," she said, moving out of Brandon's embrace and wiping her eyes quickly. "You can wait for me inside."

"So I don't need to punch him or anything?"

Grace leaned around Brandon and glared at her friend. "Seriously? Five minutes ago you were catching his shirt and offering to dance with him. It's a little late to defend my honor."

Siobhan being Siobhan, she just shrugged with a grin. "I have a mob mentality, what can I say? Okay, text me if you need me. I'll be flirting with the bartender."

That sounded about right. Siobhan was always up for a good time.

Grace waited until she went back inside then she met Brandon's gaze. "She's not that great of a support animal."

He gave a soft laugh. "I guess not. Can I see a picture of our daughter? What's her name?"

"Oh, sure, of course." Grace pulled out her phone and swiped, looking for a recent photo that really showed Fallon's face. "Her name is Fallon." She found an image she liked. It was Fallon on a nature hike just the week before. She was gazing intently into the camera, a leaf held up just under her chin. She was all long dark hair and bright blue eyes. Brandon's eyes.

She turned her camera around and showed him. "She loves nature. She likes to collect leaves."

"Oh my God..." Brandon's face leeched of color. "She looks like me. And you. She looks like me and you together."

"She does." Which was very weird, Grace had to say.

"She's beautiful."

Grace went into her camera roll and found another shot where Fallon was leaning against her hip, grinning. She was flashing the peace sign. Grace showed it to Brandon.

He moved his hand like he wanted to take her phone. "May I?"

"Sure." She gave him her phone and watched him enlarge the photo. Pride swelled through her as he studied Fallon. Her daughter was a beautiful soul, funny and compassionate and inquisitive.

Brandon shook his head, like he couldn't believe what he

was seeing. "Do you have time to go somewhere and talk? After I put a shirt on?"

She nodded. "Sure." She was actually kind of stunned at how well he was handling this. She'd never thought much beyond the moment she told him the truth. There was no plan for what happened now. "I'm staying in a hotel but there isn't much of a lobby. Is there a diner around here or anything?"

Beaver Bend was a much smaller town than she had been expecting. There weren't a lot of restaurants, bars, or hotels and there was no way they could have a deep conversation inside of Tap That.

"I rented a house for the weekend. Are you comfortable coming over? If not, tomorrow for sure, but honestly, I don't think I can sleep tonight. I really want to talk now."

Grace bit her lip. She didn't have a good reason to say no other than she was uncomfortable being alone with him because she was just as attracted to him now as she had been nine years ago. She wanted to maintain control of herself and not break down in front of Brandon. "Don't you have to finish the show?"

He gave her a look. "Do you honestly think I can go back in there and shake my junk when I just found out I have a daughter I never knew about? I know you don't know me, but trust me, I am not *that* good at compartmentalization."

Grace was shocked to find out she could not object to a single thing Brandon had said so far. Other than she wasn't sure she believed his claim he'd given her the right phone number. "Fair enough. Am I going to be able to get back to my hotel tonight? Does Lyft work here?"

"Grace. I can drive you back to the hotel."

That flustered her and she wasn't even sure why other than she was used to thinking of him as a douchebag playboy and the recent pictures she'd seen of him on social media hadn't really given her a different perspective. Now she didn't know what to think of him. "Okay."

But then they went back into the bar and instead of him just grabbing his shirt and leaving out a back door, he let himself get drawn into chatter with various women. They were stopped every two feet by someone wanting a picture with him or wanting to gush about how amazing he was to do this for charity.

"We should hang out," one woman said to him, giving him a sly smile. She had enormous breasts that were bursting out of her low-cut cotton shirt.

"Sure, I'll text you," he said.

Feeling like a third wheel, the thumping music starting to give her a headache, Grace kept on pushing her way through the crowd. So, Brandon couldn't concentrate on dancing, but he could make plans for a hookup? He clearly wasn't *that* distracted.

The fact that she even cared or had any sort of opinion also flustered her. He had shown interest in Fallon and he wanted to talk to her. That was the best she could possibly hope for. It was a super positive outcome of what could have gone horribly wrong. He could have been the asshole who questioned if he was even the father or he could have asked her what the hell he was supposed to do about it now. All scenarios she had considered as very real possibilities.

She had no right to be offended if he wanted to chat up women who thought he was the sexiest suit in Beaver Bend.

Siobhan was right at the bar where she had said she would be. She was sipping a craft beer and talking to the bartender.

"Hey," Grace said, slipping into the stool next to her. "Sorry to interrupt." She gave an apologetic smile to the bartender.

"No worries," he said. "I shouldn't be standing around

anyway. It's a busy night." He stuck his hand out. "I'm Sullivan, by the way. I own this place with my father."

Grace shook his hand. "I'm Grace. It's nice to meet you." If she wasn't mistaken this was the guy whose wife had died. She kind of hoped Siobhan wasn't planning to have sex with the widower on the night of his charity event in honor of his wife. The timing seemed just a little... yuck.

Sullivan moved away and Grace debated if she even cared enough to call Siobhan out. Her head hurt. She rubbed her temples and wondered if a glass of wine would relax her or make everything way worse. "Brandon and I are going to go to his place and talk. He was very receptive to the news and he wants to know more about Fallon. Can you get back to the hotel okay?"

Siobhan tucked her head hair behind her ear and ran her finger around the rim of her glass, eyeing Grace. "Are you sure you should go home with him? What if he murders you so he doesn't have to deal with Fallon?"

Grace almost fell off her stool. "Oh my God, Siobhan! That's insane."

"It could happen."

"I'm not asking him for anything! I don't want money."

"People panic. I'm just saying. I watch crime TV."

Grace shook her head. She loved Siobhan but she might not have been the best choice for this trip. Then she pictured her brother punching Brandon and realized Siobhan was the lesser of two evils. "Aren't you planning to go home with the bartender, who is a total stranger? How do you know he won't kill you? And remember, I went home with Brandon once before and he didn't murder me."

"That is a valid point." Siobhan sipped her beer. "And I'm not going home with Sullivan. I'm going home with his father." She pointed to the end of the bar. "He just doesn't know it yet."

"His *father*?" Grace momentarily forgot about her own situation as she turned to see where her friend was pointing. "Oh, whoa." The guy at the end of the bar was tall, broad-shouldered, and loaded with tattoos. He had salt-and-pepper hair and a full beard. He was wearing a dark blue dress shirt with the sleeves rolled up to his elbows and tight dark jeans. "He doesn't look like your type." He was also somewhere in the neighborhood of fifty.

"He's totally not interested in me. That makes him my type."

That made Grace laugh. Siobhan did tend to go for guys who just weren't into her. It was like she had to prove she could make them like her. "Well, good luck to you then." She had to admit, she was glad Siobhan wasn't flirting with Sullivan the widower tonight of all nights.

A hand spanned her back and she jumped. She wasn't used to a man just touching her at random. It was Brandon, his shirt back on and buttoned up. "Are you ready to leave or did you want to stay awhile?" he asked.

"We can leave." She wanted to get the rest of this conversation over with. There were going to be awkward questions on both of their parts.

"Great." He raised his hand to Sullivan and gestured for him to come over. "Grace, what do you drink? I'll get us something to go."

"Isn't that illegal? Open container?"

"I'm planning to buy the whole bottle of whatever you want." He looked at her like that was one, obvious. Two, no big deal.

It would have never even occurred to her you could buy a bottle of anything at a bar. "I wouldn't mind a little wine."

"Red or white?"

"White."

"Sweet or dry?"

"Somewhere in between?" She didn't mean it to be a question, but somehow her voice created the inflection that made her sound unsure. Maybe because she wasn't sure around Brandon. She considered herself a strong, independent woman but there was something about him that made her... quiet. She didn't like it. "I like Pinot Grigio," she added.

"Got it."

Sullivan came over and he and Brandon went through a list of wines Tap That had unopened. He ended up buying a sixty-dollar bottle of wine, which seemed a little excessive. At home, Grace got the $4 bottle from the neighborhood bodega and was perfectly happy with it.

Siobhan clearly thought so too because she slapped Grace's knee and gave her wide eyes. Grace just shook her head slightly.

Brandon ordered himself a two-hundred-dollar bottle of bourbon.

Once both bottles were in brown paper bags, he turned to her. "Ready?"

For a split second, Grace wanted to run away.

Because when she saw him there, bottles of liquor displayed behind him, a smile on his face, she felt eighteen years old again.

She could remember exactly how she'd felt that night. Charmed. Taken in by him.

But then she lifted her chin. She wasn't that naïve girl anymore. She was in control.

"I'm ready."

She wouldn't have come to Beaver Bend if she wasn't.

THREE

BRANDON OPENED the passenger door of his Mercedes for Grace. He had a million questions for her, and he wasn't even sure where to start. His emotions were a tornado swirling around at high speed. He was in shock. In awe that he had a daughter. And wracked with guilt that Grace had been a single parent because in a moment of careless youth he'd given her a fake name and apparently an illegible phone number.

Tossing the liquor by Grace's feet, he went around the front of his car and got in. He started the engine and turned to her. "Do you still live in Minneapolis?"

His brain was already speeding ahead, wondering if and when he could meet Fallon. It was Grace's decision, he understood and respected that, but he wanted to meet his daughter in person. He had figured someday he would have children but it wasn't something he thought about frequently. That was for later. Or so he'd thought. It was utterly bizarre to think he'd already created a child and had no clue.

"Yes." She nodded and reached for her seatbelt.

"Who is Fallon with right now, your parents?" He hoped she had a good support network.

"My brother. My parents died when I was a kid. We were raised by our grandmother but she passed away two years ago."

Damn, not what he'd been hoping to hear. "I'm sorry."

"Thanks." Her voice was soft.

"So your brother lives near you?"

"Yes, about twenty minutes away. Juan wanted to come with me but I was afraid he would punch you."

That made him laugh. "If he had, I would deserve it." He pulled out of the parking lot, grateful the house he'd rented wasn't that far from downtown. He was antsy to sit across from Grace and figure out what the hell all of this meant. "What do you do for a living?"

"I do closed captioning. Mostly from English to Spanish. It's a great job because I can do it at home. I mean, it's not necessarily exciting but it's very flexible."

He remembered then talking to her that night about her major, her plans. "Oh, that's right. You told me you were a Spanish studies major at the University of Minneapolis. I'm glad to hear that you used your degree." He also remembered telling her to say something dirty and sexy to him in Spanish and how she'd blushed and looked down, before murmuring something in Spanish, glancing up at him from under long lashes.

He'd kissed her then, cupping her cheeks and falling into the sweetness of that mouth of hers.

"I only managed an associate's degree. Fallon was born my sophomore year and I busted my ass to finish that second semester but then I needed to get a job."

Yep. Guilt pressed down on him. "I'm impressed," he said, because he was. She'd only been eighteen or nineteen if he remembered correctly.

"I did what I had to do." She shrugged, like it was no big deal.

"I'll pay you child support," he said. He owed her for the last eight years and from here on out.

But Grace made a sound of exasperation. "I didn't come here for money."

"I know that," he said, even though he didn't. But he didn't want to offend her. He would talk to his lawyer on Monday. Like it or not, she was getting financial help from him. It was the fucking least he could do.

"You don't know anything," Grace said, snapping at him. Then she sighed. "I'm sorry. This is just... hard."

He pulled into the driveway of his rental house and parked the car. He turned to her, reaching out and brushing her hair back. She pulled away. "Hey. It's okay. You can snap at me all you want. You have every right. You're calling the shots here. Whatever you want, whatever you need, I'm cool with it. But I would like to meet my daughter and I would like to contribute. And I think if you didn't want that for Fallon, you wouldn't be here in the first place, am I right?"

She nodded, biting her lip. "It was one thing when I didn't know who you were but I couldn't live with myself if I didn't tell you now. Me and Fallon, we'll be fine no matter what. But I thought I should give you the opportunity to be involved if you want to be."

There was no question what he wanted. "I want to meet Fallon. I want to be involved to the extent that I can be, given I live in Chicago and she doesn't know me."

Grace gave him a rueful look. "I have to say, after seeing your playboy lifestyle I wasn't sure what to expect. A kid doesn't exactly fit into partying in Ibiza."

It felt like an insult. It was the truth, yet he could hear the implied condemnation. She'd been a struggling single mom and he'd been a playboy bachelor. It made him feel defensive. He hadn't known so how was he at fault for partying and flashing cash?

"I wasn't planning to take Fallon clubbing," he said. "Though I wouldn't mind seeing *you* in a bikini on the beach."

Flirting was his defense mechanism. It always had been.

Grace was probably, no, definitely, the last woman he should flirt with, but he couldn't help himself. He was on emotional overload and he was attracted to her. In a weird way, even more so now that he knew she was a fucking baller who had raised his kid alone.

Her finger came out and pointed it at him. "Do not do that. Hell no, Brandon. We have to think about Fallon. No flirting, no innuendos. No touching."

His eyebrows shot up. "Wow, you went straight to touching. You're two steps ahead of me."

She blushed and shook her head. "Stop it. I'm serious. By the way, can I assume you're single since you were taking numbers at the bar and your social media is littered with hot girls?"

Grace did it again. She made him feel defensive. He also had a thought and it was one he didn't like. "Yes, I'm single. Are you? Have you ever been married?" Maybe another man had been a huge influence in Fallon's life. That would suck.

"I've never been married. And I'm single. It's not exactly easy to date as a single mom and I am not interested in having men come and go out of my daughter's life."

That made him happier than it should. "Okay. I respect you a lot for that, Grace. It can't be easy to always put someone else first."

"It's easier than you would think."

Again, that felt like a bit of a dig, but maybe he was just feeling guilty. "Can we go in the house now?"

Grace took a deep breath. "Sure."

He intended to open her door for her but she was out and on the walkway before he could get there. Grace didn't carry a purse, which he found fascinating. Her phone was tucked in her back pocket, a rectangular bump covering that tight small ass of hers. Her legs were a million miles long as she walked in front of him.

Damn it.

He had to start thinking of her as a mother. Not as a woman. Because he was just as attracted to her now as he had been nine years ago.

Grace was a mother. The mother of his child. His daughter. A *mother*. She was a mother, raising a little girl.

He chanted that in his head over and over, hoping it would have an impact on his dick.

Entering the code into the keypad on the front door he pushed it open, letting her enter before him.

"Wow, this is a beautiful house," she said.

"It's pretty cool, isn't it?" he asked, grateful for the distraction. "You should see the back of it. It's all glass overlooking the lake. The owner is only here for like a month out of the year and then rents it the rest of the time."

"Must be nice to have money to waste," Grace said, moving into the open concept kitchen and family room.

The house was contemporary, a mix of wood and metal and decorated in neutrals with lots of texture. The star was the woods surrounding three sides and the lake on the back of the house. The interior was meant to fade in contrast to nature. Brandon had stayed here twice before because he thought it was such a cool place.

"I think it's an investment for the owner," he said. "More than it is wasting money." Not that he wanted to discuss financial opportunities with her. "I could stay with my parents when I come here but that makes me feel like I'm seventeen.

They left my bedroom exactly the way it was when I graduated."

She didn't respond, just wandering around looking at the house, before going to the sliders and pulling it open to step out onto the deck. Brandon took the bourbon and the wine into the kitchen and poured them each a drink. He liked the idea of sitting outside while they talked. August in Northern Minnesota was beautiful. The perfect temperature without all that oppressive humidity he had in Chicago.

Grace was leaning over the deck railing, staring down at the lake when he stepped outside. "I brought you a glass of wine."

She took the glass from him and sipped. "This view is amazing." She breathed deeply. "The air is so clean. Fallon would love it here. I think I mentioned she loves nature and we live in an apartment. No yard or anything. This would be her happy place."

Brandon leaned over the railing next to her, swirling the liquor in his glass. "So bring her here." He had no plan, he was just spit-balling based on what she was saying. "Stay in this house with her for a few days so I can meet her, with you around, and we would have something to do. Hiking, swimming, fishing." If Fallon loved being outdoors it would be a good icebreaker. He didn't want it to be anymore awkward than it would inevitably be.

Grace turned to him, sipping her wine.

She was doing that thing again, that was burned into his memory banks. The under-the-lashes watching him. "I have to be honest with you. The thought of that terrifies me. But that's why I came here. To tell you about Fallon and give her what she's always wanted— a father. So why am I trying to think up an excuse to say no to you?"

He didn't know. Other than this was all confusing as hell

and a total realignment of both of their lives. "You shouldn't even try to say no to me," he teased. "I'm very persuasive."

Grace snorted. "That's what got us here in the first place, Jeff."

He should let it go. Focus on Fallon. But he couldn't help himself. "I hope you don't regret that night. Because I don't." His whole world had shifted but now he wanted nothing more than to get to know his daughter and her mother.

"How could I regret it?" she asked softly. "Fallon is everything to me."

He could see her love for her daughter. Her eyes were shining with love and her voice rang with sincerity. It made him want to make everything as right as he could possibly make it. "Bring Fallon here to Beaver Bend. I know I don't have a right to ask you for anything but let me try to make this easier from here on out."

She ran her fingers through her hair and turned back to the lake view. "Ugh, okay. When did you want to do this?"

"Tomorrow?" He could rearrange his next week's schedule and stay here in Beaver Bend.

"Geez, you don't waste time, do you?" Grace looked anything but happy.

"I have a lot of time to make up for," he said. He didn't think it would help his case to point out he liked instant gratification or that he usually got what he wanted. Grace already wasn't sold on his character.

"I'll talk to my brother. Maybe he can drive Fallon up here. Otherwise I'll have to go back and get her. Do you even know if we can stay in this house?"

"I'm sure it won't be a problem." Money solved a lot of life's inconveniences. He'd pay out of the nose if he had to. "Thank you, Grace. I really appreciate this."

Brandon leaned over and kissed her temple. He meant it as

they were in this together from here on out. As a symbol of his appreciation, and what they shared— a daughter.

"You won't regret this," he said.

GRACE ALREADY DID. She turned to Brandon, her cheeks flushed from a whole range of emotions. "No touching, remember?"

She couldn't think straight when he touched her. Which made her angry. And anger was a much easier emotion to hold onto and hide behind than the half a dozen other ones she was feeling at the moment.

Brandon wasn't anything like the selfish guy she'd been expecting. She'd anticipated a charmer, a bit of an emotional con artist, if she were honest with herself. But this was much more disarming. He seemed genuine. Earnest. Sure, he was a little flirtatious, but he was being pretty damn respectful. Asking her, not making demands.

"That wasn't a touch-touch," he said, though he did raise his free hand in surrender. "That was just a friendly touch."

She didn't know why, but that flustered her. The idea of being partners with him was disconcerting. "Let's just stick to a firm policy of hands off."

"That was my lips, not my hands."

Grace shot him her mom look. The one that made Fallon scramble to comply. It didn't have the same effect on Brandon.

He just laughed. "I like loopholes."

"I'm not even responding to that." She pushed off the railing and went to one of the deck chairs. Pulling her phone out of her back pocket, she sat down and sipped her wine. She had a text from Siobhan.

Status update.

Me or you?

Both. Me, sitting at bar alone, being ignored by hot dad. Whose name is Liam. You?

Agreed to let Brandon meet Fallon.

Whoa.

That summed it up completely.

Text me when you get back to the hotel safely.

Siobhan sent her a thumbs-up emoji.

Brandon sat down in the chair next to her. "Tell me about Fallon. Does she do okay in school?"

Grace nodded. "She's a great student, actually. She loves everything but gym class. She's not at all athletic, which is kind of surprising to me. I was always into sports." She looked over at him. "She must get her two left feet from you."

"Hey! Not true at all. I played hockey as a kid. And you've seen my dance moves. You can't deny that I'm awesome."

If that's what he wanted to call it. "I don't think that's called dancing so much as it's called showing off." She tried to picture him playing hockey and couldn't really see it. He was all charm and grins, not body checks and hard passes. "What position did you play?"

"Defenseman."

That made sense. It wasn't as physical, but more of a thinking man's position. "Interesting. I played center."

She enjoyed his reaction.

"You played hockey? Get out of here. You're like a buck ten." He scoffed, like he thought she was making it up.

"I'm fast. And I don't mind slamming into someone. I grew up with an older brother and I'm tougher than I look."

Brandon still looked skeptical. "You seriously played hockey? Where did you grow up?"

"Chicago. Waukegan, actually. And yes, I played intramural hockey until I was fourteen. I loved it." Grace slipped one leg over the other and leaned on the arm of the chair, toward Brandon. "I only stopped because my grandmother couldn't drive me anymore. Cataracts." By then Grace had been focusing on schoolwork anyway. It had been tough to give it up, but at sixteen she started a job, and life went on.

"I feel like I need to see this to believe it."

Grace scoffed. "I bet I can outskate you."

"Doubtful. But I'd love to see it."

She would love to knock him on his ass, that's what. Brandon was charming, but he was also arrogant. "Anytime, buddy. Bring it on." She had nine years of frustration on her side, too.

"I don't want to hurt you."

That made Grace laugh. "Or you're chickenshit. Afraid I might beat you."

Brandon sipped his drink. "Not a chance. Does Fallon play?"

"No. She doesn't like sports at all, like I said."

"Do you have any other pictures I could see? Maybe from when she was younger?"

"Sure." Grace reached for her phone. She had pictures going back at least a few years on her camera roll. She hadn't thought about bringing anything for Brandon. She'd been convinced he would be aloof.

"What's your number?" she asked. "I'll text them to you."

He rattled off his number and she chose three pictures and sent them to him, plus the current one of Fallon with the leaf. It never failed to make her heart swell when she looked at her daughter. Fallon was quiet and well-behaved, for which she was grateful every day.

Brandon pulled his phone out of his pocket and opened the images. "This just blows my mind... damn. She's beautiful, Grace."

"We did make a pretty baby," she agreed. "But more importantly, she has a beautiful soul."

Brandon turned and stared at her intently. "Do you ever wonder what it would be like if I had known?"

Grace shook her head, needing him to understand she had been forced to survive. "Not after the first year. Sure, I fantasized while I was pregnant that somehow I would find you and we'd be together. Which is ridiculous. But I was nineteen. I even went back to that bar hoping to run into you. But after Fallon was born, I gave up fantasies and got practical." She worked her ass off, even doing side jobs closed captioning porn, though she wasn't about to tell him that.

"And now?"

His bright blue eyes bore into her, disarming and raw.

"And now, what?" Grace swallowed, dismayed that her voice wobbled a little.

"Do you have a fantasy?"

That made her angry. It felt like somehow he was mocking her. Or teasing her. Or flirting. In any case, she didn't like it. "No. I don't. I don't have time for fantasies. Not everyone's life is hot tubs in Cancun." The only fun she had was the porn she watched to caption, and even that was scripted.

God, she sounded bitter. But whatever. She had been more than polite and fair to this point. There was nothing wrong with him knowing the truth. She had struggled tremendously the first few years. Money had been nonexistent and she'd been exhausted and in over her head and it was only in the last year or so she had managed to climb out of that financial hole and onto stable ground.

But Brandon didn't seem offended by the sharp tone in her voice. "Tell me your fantasy," he murmured. "And I'll make it come true. You've earned that and then some."

What the hell was he even talking about? Was he coming on

to her? Or saying she could take a vacation on his dime? Whatever he meant, it flustered the shit out of Grace. She shifted in her seat and crossed her legs together even more tightly. Her body knew what fantasy it wanted her to act on.

Her and Brandon, sex 2.0. As sober adults.

That's what her body wanted, nipples hardening under his gaze, inner thighs heating from the inside out.

Her head knew that was the dumbest thing she could ever admit to.

"I don't know what you mean," she said. "I just told you I don't have any fantasies."

Yet, unbidden, she had an image leap into her head. Of her in bed with Brandon. Having hot, dirty, unbridled sex.

The traitorous thought had her jumping up out of her chair, panicked. Oh, God, she hadn't learned a damn thing, had she?

"Where are you going?" he asked.

"I need to call my brother. He's probably worried." She started for the house.

"If you want privacy you can stay out here," Brandon said, rising from his own chair and giving a stretch that made her look away.

"Are you sure?"

"Of course." He moved past her and reached out, then stopped himself. "Right. No touching. Sorry."

She both desperately needed that rule and hated it at the same time. "I'll only be a few minutes. I need to talk to him about bringing Fallon up here."

"I understand. Let me know if you need anything." Brandon went into the house and closed the door behind him.

Grace called Juan, even though it was closing in on eleven.

"Hey, what's up?" he said as a greeting. "Did you run the bastard to ground?"

"Yes, I did. And he's being very polite and interested.

Considering I appeared out of nowhere to tell him he has a daughter he's being pretty reasonable."

"It wouldn't be out of nowhere if he had told you the truth nine years ago."

Grace glanced back to the house, lowering her voice. She wasn't sure how well sound traveled. "That is very true. But a moot point now. How is Fallon, by the way?"

"She's fine. We went to the park and then got ice cream. She's sleeping."

"Thanks. I appreciate everything you and Mina do to help me." Grace's throat constricted. After Juan had gotten out of the military when Fallon was two, he had chosen to settle in Minneapolis to be near her and help out. She owed a lot to her brother.

"You're welcome. So now what?"

"Brandon wants to meet Fallon." She held her breath. Juan wasn't going to embrace this idea. "So, I need you to bring her here."

"Fuck that." Juan sounded as outraged as she had expected. "If he wants to meet her he can fly his fancy ass to Minneapolis."

"But this will feel like a vacation to her. It's a small town, lots of trees, lots of things to do outdoors. I'm worried if Brandon comes to our place, she'll feel unsafe. Like there's a stranger in our world. We have a rigid routine and life there."

"He *is* a stranger." There was a pause, then a deep sigh. "What am I supposed to tell her? I'm not telling her the truth. That's your job."

"I know." It sounded like Juan was caving. "Just bring her and I'll tell her."

"I don't know about this, Grace. This sounds risky as fuck."

"Trust me." She knew her daughter. This wasn't going to be easy, but Fallon had been begging to meet her father for years. But if it went horribly wrong, Grace didn't want that memory to be entrenched in their apartment, in their day-to-day life.

"Is he around now?"

"Yes." Crap. He was going to ask to talk to him.

"Put him on the phone."

"No." God only knew what Juan would say to Brandon.

"Then I'm not bringing Fallon."

Damn it. She knew he meant it. "Hang on." She opened the slider and tentatively called into the dark house, "Brandon?"

"I'm right here." He put his flashlight feature on on his phone, revealing him on the couch. "Is everything okay?"

"My brother wants to talk to you."

"Okay." He stood up, flicked a light on and reached for her phone. "What's his name again?"

"Juan." Grace said a silent prayer and thrust the phone at him.

"Hey, Juan, it's a pleasure to meet you," Brandon said, sounding cool and confident.

Like a businessman.

Grace shoved her hands in the pockets of her shorts and held her breath.

"I understand. Yep. Got it." Brandon paused.

She wished she knew what her brother was saying.

"I completely understand your concerns and I'll do my best to alleviate them over the next few weeks and months. I want to be a part of Fallon's life."

He sounded like he was at a meeting discussing the budget. Grace knew Juan was not going to react positively to that.

She could actually hear his voice raised in anger, though she couldn't understand specific words.

Brandon's jaw set, like something had pissed him off. "Look. You can call me an asshole all you want, but that doesn't change the facts. I'm Fallon's biological father and I am going to be as involved as Grace allows me to be."

This was going well. Not.

"Maybe we can all just focus on Fallon and start off on the right foot."

Her brother responded and Grace held out her hand. "Just give me the phone back, Brandon."

He shook his head at her. *I've got it*, he mouthed to her. "I respect you wanting to protect your sister, man, and I appreciate all you've clearly done for her. I accept full responsibility for being an idiot when I met Grace. If you want to knock me out, you have every reason to. So how about you take one swing at me, and then we move forward?"

Grace gasped. "What? Stop it. Give me the phone."

He shook his head again. "Got it. Okay, see you tomorrow then. Thanks, have a good night."

Brandon ended the call and handed her the phone. "Why did you hang up?" she asked, outraged. "And why did you offer to let my brother punch you?"

"He said he'll call you in the morning. And it's a guy thing, don't worry about it. He hits me, we move on."

"That's a stupid thing, not a guy thing."

He just shrugged. "Trust me on this."

Because she had so much reason to trust him? "I'm skeptical."

"Hey, listen, do you mind staying here tonight? I think I drank too much bourbon while you were on the phone."

Grace's eyes widened. "Yes, I mind!" She couldn't stay here, alone, when he looked at her and reminded her of when she had been an impetuous teen.

"Why, if you're planning to stay here tomorrow with Fallon. What difference does it make?"

It made all the difference in the world. "You're not staying here with us, are you? You never said that. You said we could stay here."

"Of course I'm staying here. How else am I supposed to spend time with Fallon? We only have a couple of days, right?"

She nodded. She could do a little work here if need be, that was the beauty of her job. "I can probably swing a week, ten days tops. And school starts in a few weeks anyway."

In the dim light of the single lamp, he moved closer to her. "Then I want to stay here, with you. I want every minute I can have. Including tonight."

Alarm bells went off in her. "What do you mean?" She held her phone to her chest, like it would protect her from him touching her.

"I want to know everything about you. Everything about Fallon. I don't want you to leave. That's what I mean."

"We'll have plenty of time to talk," she said, weakly. God, she wanted him to take her in his arms and kiss her, and she hated that.

What the actual hell was wrong with her? She should be punching him like Juan wanted to.

"I just found out I have a daughter I didn't know anything about. I don't want to be alone, Grace. Stay with me."

She was drowning in his blue eyes. He cupped her cheeks, like he had all those years ago, and she knew what he was going to do. He actually was going to kiss her.

There was no way she could let him do that. Her emotions were running too high.

She'd end up having sex with him and pregnant all over again.

With every ounce of practicality she had gained as an adult, she pulled herself out of his touch. "No."

Then she pulled up a car service app on her phone.

He didn't say another word. He just walked her to the door

of the car, spoke to the driver, and gave her a "Goodnight. Talk to you tomorrow."

Part of her wanted him to stop her. To coax her to stay. She should be pleased he was letting her go, but a secret desire deep down inside of her wanted him to talk her into being wild. Into letting the old Grace, hell, the *real* Grace come out and play just for one night. The Grace who body slammed boys on the ice and who danced all night at a bar. The Grace who rode her bike with her hands off the handlebars and lay on the grass at the park gazing up at the clouds.

But he didn't stop her and thirty minutes later she was in her hotel room, alone.

Siobhan had bagged the bartender's father, much to both of their amazement, according to her friend.

Grace sat on the bed, back against the headboard, knees pulled to her chest. "It sucks being a grown-up," she muttered out loud in the dark room. "It just really fucking sucks."

FOUR

"SOMEONE BETTER BE DEAD," Rick said, when he answered his phone. "It's after midnight, Blackwell."

Brandon was back on the deck, staring out at the lake, sipping his second bourbon. He had lied to Grace. He could have driven her back to the hotel. He'd only had a couple of sips before that. He had just wanted her to stay. But she'd called his bluff and he'd let her.

Now he couldn't sleep, his head spinning in vicious circles. "I know it's late, I'm sorry. But I need you to come over. Some serious shit went down tonight."

"Are you crazy? I'm in bed. With my wife. Who is naked."

He rubbed his temples. "Did you see that woman at the bar? The brunette I left with?"

"Yes. What, did she shiv you or something?" Rick sounded more amused than concerned.

"No. She told me I have a daughter."

It still blew his mind. But now that the initial shock had worn off, he was excited. He also had no clue what he was doing. None. Rick had been raising his sister for almost ten years. He could give him some advice.

"Excuse me? Do you know her? Do you think it could be true?"

Did he know her? That was a complicated question. But he did think it was true. "Do you remember my twenty-first birthday?"

"Vaguely. Mostly I remember puking my guts out the next day after drinking seven different kinds of liquor in one night like an idiot."

"I went home with a girl. To her dorm room."

"I guess I remember that. Sort of."

"This is her. And she has an eight-year-old daughter that looks like me."

"Holy fuck."

"Exactly. You need to get your ass over here. I can't be alone tonight. This is serious shit. Mega shit."

There was rustling as Rick was clearly getting out of bed. "Give me twenty minutes."

"Thanks, man." He had known he could count on his friend.

He repeated the call with Jesse, Axl, and Sullivan. Jesse felt sorry for him. It was probably his personal worst nightmare, being a pro athlete. Axl was prosaic, as usual. Sullivan was sympathetic in that Brandon had missed Fallon's early years. He was also a little too interested in Grace for Brandon's comfort.

"She's hot," was what he actually said.

"Yes, she is. I have fucking good taste," Brandon said, crossing his ankles on the ottoman he had dragged over in front of his deck chair. "But you don't need to be looking at her."

It was hard to hear because Sullivan was behind the bar, talking on his cell, but his friend's interest had come across loud and clear.

"I can come over but I'll be late. I have to stay here until close because my dad went upstairs with your Baby Mama's friend."

That made Brandon laugh. "Shut the fuck up. She's younger than us." Sullivan's dad was not known for dating, let alone hookups. The night was full of surprises.

"She was younger than us and relentless. I kind of feel bad for the old man. She practically dragged him upstairs by his dick."

Brandon snorted. "Right. By the way, don't ever say Baby Mama again. I hate that phrase."

"What the hell am I supposed to call her?"

"Grace."

"Where's the fun in that?"

"Sorry to disappoint you. See you when you can get here."

They ended the call and Brandon called his lawyer.

"I know it's late," he started.

"It's midnight. That's more than late."

"Sorry. But so, listen, what are child support laws in Minnesota? I just found out I have an eight-year-old daughter. I want to pay the mother back support."

His lawyer, Dave, whistled. "Damn. That's a kick in the dick. And is she asking for back support? Because that's going to be quite a hit to the wallet. It's a standard formula based on your income, which has been increasing every year. There is no negotiating it. You're going to owe her well over six figures."

It was just money. It didn't change anything. But it would make life easier for Grace and his daughter. "That's fine. Whatever number you come up with, double it, and let me know. I'll be in touch next week."

"You're not obligated to pay her back support if she never filed for it. Just support moving forward. And as your attorney, I'm going to advise you to get a DNA test."

"I'm not doing that." He could see himself in Fallon. Besides, he believed Grace.

"Then I'm going to advise you you're an idiot."

"That's what I pay you for. I acknowledge your point but I'm not changing my mind."

He didn't think Grace was exactly rolling in cash. She most likely lived on a budget. Even if she didn't want to spend the money now, it could pay for Fallon to go to college.

After Dave, he called his assistant, George, who had amazing research skills, and was a tech whiz. George was in his early twenties and he answered the call, club music pounding behind him. "Hang on, going outside."

Brandon waited, mentally acknowledging George was him ten years ago. He resisted the urge to ask George if he had quality condoms on him. "I need you to cancel everything next week. I need to stay in Beaver Bend for at least a week. Maybe two."

"Seriously? Sure, done, but that's going to push a lot of projects back."

"I just found out I have a daughter who is eight. Rearrange everything."

There was a long pause. George finally said, "Oh, shit. Okay, sure." He sounded buzzed.

Brandon would have to schedule a reminder to make sure George was on it starting tomorrow.

All that done, Rick and Axl arrived right on each other's heels. Jesse minutes later.

Jesse's hair was sticking up in all directions as he entered the house. "Dude. I left that chick's bed to come over here. That's how much I fucking love you."

"What girl?" The earlier part of the night, pre-Grace, was a blur.

"The one who was wearing my jersey. She was *really* excited to be hanging out with me."

"I don't even remember her." He didn't. "Come out on the deck. Sullivan's hung up at the bar. Apparently, his dad is banging the redhead."

"Liam is banging a redhead? I didn't see that one coming," Axl said.

"Me either. And hey, I left my naked wife behind. I should get props too," Rick said.

"My girlfriend was going down on me," Axl said. "I win the best friend award."

"So, what have we learned?" Brandon asked wryly, as he pulled three glasses down out of the kitchen cabinet. "Everyone was getting laid tonight, including Sullivan's *dad*, but me. Got it."

"That is sad," Jesse said.

"Sullivan isn't having sex, if that makes you feel any better," Rick said.

"Not really. He's at work. If he wasn't, who knows what he'd be doing?" He poured the bourbon generously, trying to erase thoughts of what it would feel like to sink inside Grace. She was really sexy. Even more so because now he knew she was tough as nails. So beautiful and a fighter. "Grab a glass and come outside. I can't sleep. My head feels like it's going to explode."

They all settled into chairs on the deck and sipped the bourbon.

"So what the hell happened?" Axl said. "One minute you're dancing, then you just disappeared."

"She told me on that damn stage. It took me a second to remember her, I'm not going to lie. That was a long time ago and I was drunk. Plus, it was just all out of context."

"Why would she tell you onstage in the middle of a charity

strip show eight or nine years after the fact?" Rick asked. "It seems like fucked-up timing."

"She never told me because she didn't know who I was. Remember we all used fake names that night? I told her I was Jeff Spicoli." Brandon winced at the memory. That had been an asshole thing to do. Sure, it was one thing to talk to random girls at the bar and give a bullshit name but he should have confessed to Grace the truth before he took her pants off. She probably would have laughed about it.

If he had, he might not have missed the first eight years of Fallon's life. He took a huge swallow and let the bourbon burn down his throat. The neighbor had peacocks and he heard one of the birds let out a cry in the dark. The sound annoyed his already strung-out nerves.

"I don't even know what the fuck to say to that," Jesse said. "Other than damn, that sucks."

"Yep." Brandon stared out into the darkness. He couldn't see the lake, no matter how much he strained his eyes. The clouds had shifted and were blocking the moonlight.

"You can sit around and kick your own ass or you can just go from here," Rick said. "I take it Grace is open to you being in your daughter's life? That's a cool thing, bro. You have a daughter."

Brandon pulled his phone out and passed it to Axl, who was immediately to his right. "This is Fallon."

Axl whistled. "She looks like you." He showed the other guys.

"I know. It's a complete mind fuck." He glanced over at his friends. "I'm fucking terrified to meet her. Grace's brother is bringing her here tomorrow. I'm excited, but terrified. How do I explain that I lied to her mother?"

"Listen," Rick said. "I have a lot of experience with a father who just does whatever the fuck he wants and all three of us kids are still in his life. He pisses me off but even I tolerate him. Rachel is old enough that she knows the score and she'd rather have him than no parent at all because he does love us. River is a genius and even she overlooks his flaws and forgives him because kids are adaptable. And kids want one thing— to be loved by their parents."

That actually made him feel a lot better. "You think so? Grace did say Fallon has always wanted to meet her father."

"Then you're good," Sullivan said. "The kid is predisposed to like you. You might want to work on the mom though. She doesn't have a lot of reasons to be on your side."

Brandon shot Sullivan a look. "Great. Something else to worry about." Though he didn't think Grace hated him. She had every right to, but she seemed determined to be practical about the whole thing. She clearly just wanted what was right for Fallon.

"If I were you, I'd lay off the bourbon," Axl said. "You don't want to face this meeting hungover."

Axl had a point. Brandon shoved his glass at Jesse. "Here. You finish this."

Grace had texted him she thought Fallon would be there around noon. He had less than twelve hours before the biggest meeting of his entire adulthood. There was no research or prep he could do to ensure he made a good impression.

He would just have to approach it the way he did everything in the business world— with confidence and a smile.

And hope like hell that would be good enough.

"THE KID IS LIT," Juan said, as Fallon opened the car door a split second after he put his car in park. "Maybe we should have eased her into this, Grace."

Grace heard her brother, but she was more concerned with

hopping out of the car and following her daughter, who was running pell-mell across the lawn of Brandon's rental house. Fallon had arrived with Juan at Grace's hotel and she had sat her down and tried as gently as possible to explain the situation. That her biological father was here. Fallon had been thrilled.

The whole car ride over from the hotel she'd been bouncing in her seat and talking a mile a minute. Now she was down on her knees turning over a rock and looking like Grace had fed her an upper for breakfast along with her pancakes. She was so wound it was actually alarming. This had the potential to be a total disaster if Brandon was aloof or cool to Fallon. Which he might be, inadvertently, since Fallon was so high energy right now. He might balk.

"Fallon, come here. Take my hand." Grace was shaking, she was so nervous. If this hurt Fallon in any way, Grace would never forgive herself.

"Sure." Fallon abandoned the rock and ran over to her. Juan hadn't combed Fallon's hair and she looked like a wild child, curls tangled and bouncing. She was wearing overall shorts, because she was addicted to pockets. Fallon liked to put everything she found in nature in them.

Grace spent wash day pulling feathers, pebbles, blades of grass, and leaves out of Fallon's pockets.

Fallon looked up at her. "What's wrong, Mom?"

Grace took a deep breath. "I just hope you like Brandon. I'm worried. I don't want you to be disappointed."

"Why wouldn't I like him?" Fallon asked, looking genuinely puzzled. "He's my *dad*."

If only it were that simple.

"What if he doesn't like me?" Fallon slipped her hand into Grace's.

That made Grace's heart squeeze. She ran her free hand

gently over that mass of hair. "He'll like you. You're very easy to like."

Her brother came up behind them. "Even I like you, and you know I don't like anyone," he said, joking.

Fallon laughed.

"Listen to Uncle Juan. It's true." Grace looked at her brother over Fallon's head and gave him a warning look. She hadn't even wanted him to come with them but he had insisted. He had agreed to leave after fifteen minutes or so. He just wanted to be there to take them back to the hotel in case it went south right from the beginning.

"Is this a hotel?" Fallon asked, as they approached the front door.

"No, it's a house. For one family."

Her daughter's eyes widened. "It's huge. Is my dad rich?" she asked with the straight-forward manner of a kid.

Grace sighed. How the hell was she supposed to answer that? "I don't know," she lied, because she didn't want Fallon and Brandon's relationship to be about money, in any way.

Juan snorted.

She ignored her brother and rang the doorbell. She was wearing shorts and a T-shirt and now she suddenly felt like she should have dressed up or something. This was a pivotal moment. It was going to change all of their lives.

Her stomach clenched. She felt like she was going to throw up.

Brandon opened the door, dressed casually in plaid shorts and a black T-shirt.

"Hi!" she said to him, sounding demented. Her whole face had gone hot and she thought for a split second she was going to faint.

She had given up years ago on imagining this moment would ever happen and now here it was and she wanted everything to be fine. Taking a deep breath, reminding herself that she was the key in making this meeting comfortable for everyone, she blew air back out and said, "Brandon, this is Fallon. Fallon, this is Brandon. Your father."

Brandon looked awed as he stared down at Fallon. "Hi, Fallon, it's very nice to meet you. Can I give you a hug?"

Fallon had burrowed herself into Grace's side the second the door had opened. But at his question she pulled away slightly and nodded, clearly feeling shy. She gave him a loose, awkward hug. Brandon ran his hands over her hair, like he was testing to make sure she was real. For a brief second he even closed his eyes, like he wanted to remember the moment, breathe it in.

She was shocked, and touched. He opened his eyes and mouthed silently over Fallon's head to her, *thank you.*

Grace nodded, a lump in her throat.

Brandon looked like he didn't want to let Fallon go, but when her daughter pulled back he reluctantly let her go. "Come on in, everyone." He stuck his hand out to her brother. "Juan."

Her brother shook his hand but didn't say a word.

Fallon went running past Brandon to the huge glass window wall in the family room. "Mom, look at the lake! Did you see it?" She turned back, excited. "Are we really staying here? This house is so cool."

It was. Now that Grace was seeing it in the daylight, it was even bigger than she had realized. The first floor was open concept and the kitchen was gourmet. A true chef's kitchen, with a subzero fridge and an eight-burner stove. The cabinetry looked custom and expensive, as did all of the furniture. It looked like the intention had been to blend the inside with the outdoors. Everything was minimal, in neutrals, with lots of texture. It appeared to her uneducated designer's eyes that the point was to focus on the lake. It was very beautiful.

She didn't know if staying here was the right thing or not but they were all in now. Time to pull herself together and make this a decent couple of days for her daughter. "I saw it. Brandon says we can go out on the lake later. His friend has a boat. It's going to be fun."

"Do I get my own room?" Fallon asked.

Grace nodded. "Yes."

"Can I see it now?"

She looked to Brandon for that.

He was watching Fallon, but when she gave him a verbal nudge, he said, "Huh? Right. Sure. This way." He gestured to the hallway and when Fallon ran ahead of him he cleared his throat and glanced at Grace. "She seems more interested in the house than me. I guess that's better than tears, right?"

"Don't take it personally. It's just her way of processing all this." She knew her daughter well enough to know she was feeling a little uncertain. She was used to the idea of a mysterious unknown father. The reality of him was bound to be overwhelming.

He nodded. "I'm just going to roll with it."

"Perfect."

"Second door on the right," he called loudly to Fallon.

Fallon came to a quick stop and threw open the door. "Cool. I have a huge bed all to myself." She looked back at Brandon. "Where's Mom's room?"

"It better be far away from his," Juan murmured under his breath, right near her ear.

Grace swatted backwards at her brother. "Hush."

"Your mom's room is right next to yours."

Fallon turned the knob and opened that door too. She ran in then popped her head back out, hair tumbling forward. "Mom, you have a hot tub! Trade rooms with me."

Grace laughed. "No way, kid." She had no intention of

using a hot tub but she wasn't about to let her daughter have that room. She would never sleep a wink, worried somehow Fallon would drown. Her thoughts always ran to the worst-case scenario.

"Come and see it, Mom."

She obliged her daughter and went into the room. "Wow." The hot tub was in a bump-out jutting into the woods and accessible to the deck. "This is very cool."

"We'll be right back," her brother said. "I'm going to talk to Brandon for a minute then I'll take off."

Grace shot her a brother a warning look. He gave her a grin. Trying not to worry, she followed Fallon past the bed and a chaise to the hot tub. "It's like being in a treehouse, isn't it?"

Fallon nodded. "I wish we lived in a house like this."

There it was. The painful reminder that now that she had found Brandon, and he had money, Fallon was going to compare. And her mother was going to come up short in what she could give her materialistically.

Grace reminded herself that love and support were more important than possessions, but it had always been her and Fallon against the world. Now it was all going to be different.

She heard the unmistakable sound of a punch connecting with a target out in the hallway.

"What was that?" Fallon asked, frowning.

Instead of feeling like she needed to stop her brother, Grace stood still. Fist fighting was no solution to any problem, but nonetheless it gave her an unexpected smug satisfaction. "Nothing, baby. Climb in the hot tub without the water and see how big it is."

Fallon didn't hesitate. She scrambled in and stood up. "I'm queen of the world!" she said, holding her arms out. The kid had been watching Titanic over and over all summer and it clearly showed.

"Yes, you are."

Queen of Grace's world. She felt tears well in her eyes. She was so grateful for this kid.

If anything, she owed Brandon and his stupid purple party condom.

Not the other way around.

FIVE

BRANDON FOLLOWED Grace's brother down the hallway. He knew he was either going to get chewed out or punched. Juan wasn't a huge guy, but he was tall and wiry, like Grace. He did have some muscle though, like he worked hard to try to keep his narrow frame filled out.

Without warning Juan turned and raised his fist.

He didn't sucker-punch him. He waited, gave Brandon warning. "Ready?"

He nodded. "Give me what you got. I deserve it. One hit and then let's move on. I won't block it."

Juan pulled back and Brandon moved his feet, planting them apart so he wouldn't get knocked over. He was determined not to block the punch or flinch in any way. He wanted to prove he was man enough to take it. Juan nailed him with a wicked right hook.

Brandon briefly saw stars but he managed to stay standing where he was. Pain exploded in his nose and he felt the wetness of the blood streaming out of it. He stubbornly refused to grab and hold it. Playing hockey had taught him to not back down or you'll be the target over and over.

"Feel better?" he asked, shaking his head a little to clear the ringing. Damn, that fucking hurt.

"A lot better." Juan ran his knuckles down the front of his jeans. "You might want to get a towel. You're going to bleed all over this fancy fucking house."

It was starting to become pretty obvious Grace and Juan had grown up working class. As proud as Brandon was of his success, he didn't want to flash his money in front of either of them. Or Fallon. That would be insulting to Grace, who had clearly worked hard to support her daughter.

"Good idea," he said and went into the kitchen for a hand towel. Ice might not be a bad idea either. He rummaged around in the drawers, not sure where anything was.

"I'm going back to Minneapolis," Juan said, leaning on the counter, just watching him open and close random drawers. "But if you hurt my sister or my niece, I'll be back."

"I'm not going to hurt them." Brandon found a towel and unfurled it. He looked at Juan. He could feel blood running over his lips and he refused to wipe it on principle. "And for the record, I appreciate you having Grace's back. But I seriously doubt that when you were twenty or twenty-one you didn't do something stupid with a girl."

Juan rubbed his chin. "Sure, but I never got anyone pregnant."

"That you know of. You could have a ten-year-old kid walking around somewhere. Unless you were celibate, or never had a single hookup in your entire life, you can't be judging me, man." Brandon pushed the button on the fridge door and caught some ice cubes in his hand. "I'm going to do everything I can, now that I know, to do what's right for Grace and Fallon. Period."

Juan watched him for a minute, then he nodded. "That's all I need to hear. And thanks for fucking up my world view. I was in the service from eighteen to twenty-two. I don't even want to think about the shit I did."

"Probably with someone's sister." Brandon wrapped the towel around the ice cubes.

Juan let out a crack of laughter. "Damn. Probably. You're all right, Blackwell."

"Thanks. For the record, I know my way around a boardroom but I don't know jack about how to have a relationship with a kid I never knew I had. Go easy on me." He was still reeling from seeing a living human being who looked like him standing in front of him.

"Yeah, right." But Juan did stick his hand out.

Brandon shook it. "Do I need to get some suitcases out of the car?"

"Yes. Plus Grace's computer bag. Porn doesn't stop for vacation."

Brandon's hand jerked and he spilled the ice out of the towel onto the floor. "Excuse me? Porn?"

Juan looked pleased with his bombshell. "What, she didn't tell you?"

"*No.*" Was the mother of his child a porn star? Holy shit, he didn't know if that was awful or in some way weirdly hot... "What the hell do you mean?"

"She does closed captioning for porn on the side for extra money."

Relief rushed through him. Even as his traitorous asshole of a cock got hard picturing Grace naked on a bed, rolling around. Of course, he was picturing him with her, not some random dude porn star. There was something wrong with him, damn. He was a fucking pervert. "What the hell is there to caption in porn? It's all moaning."

"There are some stellar plots in porn."

"If you say so." Brandon followed Juan out to his car. "Does Grace... like doing that?"

"Watching porn?" Juan looked horrified. "I don't know. I doubt it. And now I'm sorry I brought it up. That jab backfired on me."

"It really did." Because now Juan was uncomfortable and Brandon was having some very dirty thoughts imagining Grace working at home during school hours and getting turned on watching porn. Then easing her fingers down into her shorts and...

He cleared his throat. "Well, she can quit that now if she wants. I'm giving her child support whether she likes it or not." But if she kept the side gig, he was going to want to see it. In action.

Damn it. If he had known he was going to have to be hands-off a baby mama this weekend he would have made different choices in the last few months. He'd been celibate longer than he cared to think about, preoccupied with his expansion into Asia. Now he couldn't get thoughts of Grace out of his head. He was as attracted to her as he had been nine years ago, maybe more.

Juan popped the trunk. "You really don't know my sister very well, do you? She's not going to do anything she doesn't want to. She may look scrawny and sweet, but she's neither. She's tough as nails."

He wasn't sure if that was a warning or a threat. "I never would have thought of her as scrawny. But I don't think she has a choice. Child support is court ordered."

Grace's brother just shook his head and put down two suitcases. He shoved a backpack at Brandon. "Good luck." He looked around Brandon and shouted, "Grace! I'm leaving."

"You can stay a night if you want," Brandon felt obligated to offer, even though he really wanted time alone with Fallon and Grace. "That's a long drive."

"No, thanks. I'm a plumber and you never know when you'll get an emergency call."

"Got it."

Grace appeared in the doorway. "You couldn't walk back into the house?" she asked Juan, rolling her eyes. But she walked down the drive and gave her brother a hug. "Thanks for bringing Fallon. Love you."

Fallon came tearing out of the house, much like he imagined he was at that age, and zipped around him to hug her uncle. "Bye."

Then he was getting back in the car and Grace was struggling to get both suitcases, backpack already secure on her shoulders.

"Let me help you." He tried to take both suitcases from her, but she resisted, holding on to them.

"I've got it."

Juan was right. She was stubborn. "I'm not letting you carry three bags while I stand here." He pulled again.

"I have it," she said exasperated, unrelenting.

He smiled at her, realizing he had the perfect ammunition to get her to accept his assistance. He leaned in close to her. She drew away. He leaned further and murmured, "So what's this about you watching porn for a living?"

Grace gasped and dropped her grip on the suitcase handles. "Come on, Fallon." She fast-walked back into the house, ushering her daughter.

Victory. Brandon picked up the suitcases and carried them into the house.

"You're going to have to get used to me helping you," he said.

Grace was picking up the ice he'd spilled. "Apparently, I'm going to have to get used to you being inappropriate too." She shot him a glare, her cheeks stained pink. "Little ears, you know."

He ignored that. "Fallon, do you want to go down to the lake? Did you pack a bathing suit?"

"Nope. Mine doesn't fit anymore."

Grace's head whipped around. She shot her daughter a warning look that he didn't understand.

"We can still go down there and explore."

"Cool. How do we get there?"

"There are steps from the deck."

Fallon ran with an energy that amazed him. He was going to have to up his workout regimen to keep up with this kid.

"I can afford to buy her a bathing suit," Grace murmured, shoving her hands in her pockets. "It's just there was no reason to buy one this year. We don't have a community pool."

Ah, so that's what it was. "Grace, I didn't think anything about it. Seriously. What do I know about what kids have or don't have? Nothing. But even if you couldn't afford something, I would never judge you for that."

She bit her lip.

He felt guilty teasing her about the porn. "I'm sorry about the porn comment. I wasn't trying to make you feel bad. I actually find it a hell of a turn-on."

"Oh my God." She rolled her eyes. "Just stop talking. Please."

Not yet. "I'm giving you child support. Just so you know."

Grace glanced back to see where their daughter was. "You can shove your child support up your ass," she said, her voice deceptively sweet.

He was expecting that reaction. "Use it for her to go to college. Buy a house. Hell, donate it to charity. Whatever you want. But you're taking it."

"I'd rather shove it up your ass," she said, nose wrinkling.

Brandon laughed. She was the master of the grumpy glare. He had a feeling this was what Fallon looked like when she didn't get her way. "That would require me getting naked first," he murmured. "And I don't think you want that, do you, Grace?"

Her eyes widened. "You're a wicked flirt, Jeff."

He had a feeling it was going to be a long time, if ever, before she stopped using the name Jeff to drive her point home. This time though it just amused him. "Never said I wasn't. Let's go outside before Fallon falls in the lake."

Grace started. "Is that possible? Oh my God. She wouldn't go down there without me." She was already starting to jog to the back door. "Actually, that is a stupid thing to say. Of course, she would. She wanders."

Brandon followed her. Now he was alarmed too. But Fallon was waiting for them on the deck, sitting on the steps and watching a colony of ants zipping in and out of a hole in the corner of the decking. He gave a sigh of relief. Grace's shoulders sagged. She shot him a dirty look over her shoulder, like it was his fault.

"Sorry," he said, though he wasn't sure what the hell he was apologizing for. Basically, the last nine years.

"Good girl for waiting," Grace said to Fallon, running her hand over her daughter's curls. "Ready to go to the lake?"

"Mom." Fallon rolled her eyes and stood up. "I'm not a little kid." She glanced at him for the first time in ten minutes. "She thinks I'm a baby. I'm not." She crammed her hands in the pockets of her overalls like she was embarrassed by her mother.

Or maybe like it was important she impress him. He wasn't sure. "I think that's a mom thing," he told her. "Moms worry about us because they love us."

"What do dads do?" Fallon asked.

Oh, man. That was a sledgehammer to the heart. Because hell if he knew. Her question didn't sound innocent, either. Her tone sounded accusatory. But then again, he was defensive. "They take their daughters fishing. And tell them to stay away from boys."

Grace snorted.

"There are fishing poles under the deck. Let's grab them. Do you like fishing?" he asked Fallon.

"I've only been once but I liked it."

"What's your favorite thing to do?"

"My favorite thing ever is to go to the pound and pet the dogs." Fallon was already running down the steps. She skipped the last two and jumped. "We can't have a dog in our apartment but I *love* them. They're *everything*."

He was glad to hear she liked animals. "I get that. My whole time growing up I wanted a dog and my parents said no. They didn't have a good reason, though, like your mom does. They just didn't want dog hair in the house."

Speaking of his parents, he really needed to give them a call. A previously unknown granddaughter was pretty big news.

The same thought seemed to occur to Grace. She gave him a questioning look. When Fallon took off running toward the lake, he squinted, wishing he'd grabbed his sunglasses. "I mentioned my parents still live here. I'm going to have to tell them about Fallon, but it's up to you if you want her to meet them or not. Despite being anti-dog hair, they're nice people. I had a loving, normal childhood. They would be kind to her."

Grace gave a nervous nod. "God, this is so weird, isn't it?"

"The very definition of awkward," he agreed.

"So what do we do to make it less weird?" Grace walked like her daughter, hands in her pockets. Only with Grace, it was sensual. She moved with inherent femininity and a sort of sly shyness.

She was beautiful, but it was more than that. Grace was an amazing combination of strength and vulnerability, bold and shy.

Have sex again, was his first instant response to her question.

But he knew that would only complicate the shit out of things.

At the same time, though, it would make them more comfortable around each other.

It would be better than this hands-off politeness.

It was very tempting.

It took everything he had not to say something flirtatious. He damn near bit his own tongue off restraining himself. "You tell me. You're the brains of this operation. I'm the beauty."

"Just grab your rod," she said, looking equal parts annoyed and bemused.

Brandon raised his eyebrows, waiting for her to realize what she had said.

"Oh my God, stop it!" She laughed though and it was a big, beautiful, genuine laugh. "What, are you twelve?"

"Definitely not twelve. Or even twenty-one. I know what I'm doing now."

Her cheeks turned pink. "I think you did okay at twenty-one. I didn't have any complaints until morning."

Brandon felt two things simultaneously— deep, male satisfaction and sincere regret.

What could have become of him and Grace if he hadn't been a fucking idiot?

And what could they be now? Polite strangers? Friends? Or something more?

But before he could express that thought Grace jogged after Fallon, her hair bouncing down her back. She caught up with her daughter. Their daughter. She slipped her hand into

Fallon's and Brandon realized with the utter certainty of the Titanic that his life as a playboy was sinking.

Hell, sunk.

Everything was different now. Everything.

BRANDON WAS GOOD WITH FALLON.

Grace was equal parts relieved and annoyed. It would be miserable and break her heart if Fallon reacted poorly to Brandon or if he were a heavy-handed douchebag.

He wasn't. He was patient, he was calm. He didn't tease her, which was something Fallon hated. Though he did make silly jokes that could almost be categorized as "dad" jokes. Nor did he try to force any engagement from Fallon. He seemed to inherently understand how best to handle her.

Which was awesome. And scary.

How would she feel if Fallon suddenly became a daddy's girl? Abandoned, that's how. Which was ludicrous. But irrational or not, she didn't want to lose her daughter. She didn't want to suddenly become the lame parent while Brandon was the cool one. Though hell, that was probably inevitable.

He was a charming guy. It was how she had wound up taking him back to her dorm room. That same easygoing confidence had probably contributed to his obvious financial and business success. He had good people skills.

Grace watched him help Fallon cast her line into the lake from where she sat swinging her legs over the side of the dock.

"Now what?" Fallon asked.

"We wait. If you feel a tug on your line, let me know." Brandon was next to Fallon, his long legs dangling next to hers. Their heads were bent down, studying the surface of the water.

Grace thought she was going to cry, not because she was jealous but because in one swift moment, she realized she had provided Fallon with the one thing she had always wanted— a father. Where it went from here was anyone's guess, but now that unanswered question finally had a response.

And it seemed to be a good one.

Fallon had the same nose as Brandon and in profile they looked so similar it took her breath away.

She decided she needed five minutes in the house. One, because she was going to cry and she didn't want to alarm Fallon. Two, they might benefit from a few minutes' conversation without her hovering like the neurotic mother she was.

"I'm grabbing a drink in the house," she said. "Anyone need anything?"

Brandon glanced at her over Fallon's head and smiled. "I'm good, thanks. I stocked the fridge this morning so hopefully there is something you like in there."

"I'm fine with water. Fallon, do you want anything?"

"I'll take a pop," she said, like Grace just handed her soda on a regular basis.

"Nice try," she told her daughter. "You can have water."

Fallon made a face but it seemed more from habit than anything else as she was distracted by watching the water anxiously for any sign of a fish.

Grace started down the deck. Then stopped in her tracks when she heard her daughter clearly ask, "Why did you lie to my mom?"

She should leave and give them privacy but she couldn't seem to make her feet move.

"Did you ever just have a lie pop out and you're not even sure why?" Brandon asked Fallon.

"I don't think so. I only lie when I think I'm going to get in trouble for something."

Not new information, but Grace did appreciate the confirmation. Fallon was notorious for saying she had washed her hair when all she had done was rinse it off. Something Grace could never figure out. What was the beef against shampoo? Getting dirty hair wet just made Fallon smell like a wet dog.

Curious to see how Brandon would explain nine years away, Grace listened with a surprising amount of sympathy. She had been called out by her confused daughter many times over the years and there was just no easy way to explain a hookup to a child.

She took one step forward just to make it look like she was headed to the house in case either Fallon or Brandon glanced her way.

"When I was younger, sometimes I said things because I thought they would be funny or because I just wasn't thinking. I never meant to hurt your mom," Brandon said. "Or you."

"Well, it was rude," Fallon said vehemently.

Ouch. Grace's heart hurt. For her daughter and for Brandon. A foolish moment of drunken impulse and now he had an eight-year-old calling him out.

"You're right, it was rude. I'm sorry. I really am. I'm going to try to make it up to you the best I can, Fallon. If you'll let me."

"My mom always tells me I should forgive people if they're sorry. I think I can forgive you *if* you're not a jerk from now on."

With that pronouncement, Grace rushed the rest of the way down the deck and across the grass before she started crying in earnest. As it was, she could barely see through her watery eyes. God, she was proud of her daughter. Meeting her previously anonymous father was a big-ass deal and Fallon could be throwing a fit. Or being unabashedly needy or demanding. Instead, she was approaching it very reasonably and even though they had a long road ahead of them, Grace was optimistic Fallon and Brandon could development a relationship unique to them.

Fallon was never going to live with him, but they could have a sort of friendship relationship.

Inside the house, Grace opened the fridge and pulled out three bottled waters. Brandon wasn't lying. He had loaded it up with enough food to feed Fallon's whole class. It looked like he'd experienced some panic over what Fallon might like. The items inside ranged from string cheese to sushi to cherry tomatoes to chocolate pudding. Grace was just about positive Fallon would eat a worm before she would sushi. That just wasn't going to happen.

She grabbed a bag of baby carrots and took it with her. Fallon loved them.

But when she got back to the water, Fallon waved off her offer. "I'm busy."

Grace started to sit on the deck next to her but Fallon said, "Mom. Please don't crowd me. I have a thing going on here."

Okay, then. Grace had no idea what the "thing" was but she wasn't about to argue with Fallon today of all days. "Got it."

"You can sit by me," Brandon said, giving her a wink and patting the dock on his right. "Plenty of room."

"Yeah, sit by my dad."

My dad.

Damn. Hearing that was like taking a bullet. Abrupt and painful.

On top of it all, Fallon sounded kind of bratty about it. Grace took a deep breath and reminded herself yet again, she had to be patient today, of all days. Patient as fuck. This wasn't about her. It was about Fallon.

Ignoring Brandon's wink, she sat down a good two feet away from him, dangling her long legs over the deck. It made her feel melancholy. She'd never been able to give her daughter this—these lazy summer days fishing at the lake.

She was staring out at the sun dappling the surface of the

dark water when Brandon startled her by snaking her fingers through his. She turned to reprimand him and pull away, but his expression stopped her. He looked not only compassionate, but as emotionally overloaded as she felt.

He leaned over and murmured, "This doesn't count as touching, does it?"

"No," she said, and her voice was raw. "I'll allow it." It seemed like they both needed the comfort.

He gave her a little smile. "Thanks, Judge Grace."

"That's Judge Martinez to you." She should pull her hand away, but she kept it there, tucked inside his.

He was giving her a warm look that did strange things to her insides. It reminded her of how she had felt at eighteen, life rife with possibilities. She'd been free, hopeful, a little wild. She'd seen his blue eyes and jumped off a cliff.

It felt like a million years ago and yet here he was again. It was surreal.

Dangerous.

Somewhere inside her still lived that impulsive girl.

"Something's pulling on my line!" Fallon yelled.

The moment between them was broken.

They both turned to look at Fallon.

Ironically, it was Brandon who pulled his hand away from hers.

Grace's mouth went hot and she grabbed the bottle of water she'd brought down and took a huge sip.

Brandon was a sperm donor. Nothing more. That hadn't changed.

Yet she watched him gently help Fallon reel in her line and she knew she was lying to herself.

Everything had changed.

And maybe that wasn't a bad thing.

SIX

BRANDON SAT on Axl's boat and watched Grace sitting opposite him, arm wrapped around Fallon. Both of their hair was streaming behind them as they cruised out onto the lake. Grace wasn't looking at him, but at the scenery, Fallon tucked against her chest as they both sat sideways.

It was fucking overwhelming.

And beautiful.

Grace was beautiful as a mother.

And their daughter was the perfect blend of both of them. His eyes, Grace's hair and lean frame.

"I'm freaked out just looking at her," Axl said, dropping next to him. "I can't even imagine how you feel."

Brandon glanced over at his friend. He'd known Axl since the second grade and he was level-headed and not inclined to panic. "That's not reassuring. And I can't believe you're letting Leighton drive your boat."

Axl shrugged. "She grew up on the ocean in LA. She knows her way around a boat. Besides, I trust her."

Six months ago, when Leighton had moved from LA to Beaver Bend to be with Axl, Brandon had thought they were both insane. They barely knew each other, as far as he was concerned. Axl wasn't an impulsive guy. But apparently love made people a little crazy. It seemed to be working out just fine for them though and Brandon was happy for his friend.

"She does look confident." Leighton was a petite, curvy blonde, her hair pulled back in a ponytail.

One night when they'd been hanging out, Axl had drunk too much whiskey and had talked a lot about his girlfriend's body. Like a lot. So much that Brandon had finally told him he might want to stop undressing his girlfriend for his friends to picture and enjoy. Brandon had thought it was hilarious but Axl had realized he'd spilled a little too much.

Brandon understood it a little better now. He wanted to talk indefinitely about both Grace and Fallon. He was grateful they were on the sundeck where they couldn't hear him over the engine.

"I can't ever make it up to Grace," he said now. "But she's amazing. She's done a fabulous job with Fallon, while working full-time and taking on side jobs." Captioning porn. That still was messing with his head and his dick, picturing how that went down. "It wasn't fair to her."

"She looks like she's okay with how her life has gone down. She seems like she has her shit together."

"She does." He was confident of that.

"She have a boyfriend?" Axl asked, stretching his legs out in front of him.

The thought of Grace having a boyfriend didn't sit right with him. He didn't want to be on the outs like that. He'd already missed eight years. He didn't want to be the guy who occasionally popped his head in while another guy spent multiple days a week with Fallon.

In Grace's bed.

"No boyfriend," he said. "Right now. Thank God."

"Why does it matter?" Axl's tone was deceptively casual.

Brandon knew what Axl was doing. He was trying to figure out where Brandon stood. The answer to that was he had no fucking clue where he stood.

"Because I don't want to compete with some random dude for time with Fallon. Or have her think he's the shit and I'm just some guy who looks like her who lives in Chicago." Maybe it wasn't fair of him, but hell, that's how he felt.

"I can see that. But the truth is, at one point or another Grace will have a boyfriend."

That was annoying. "Thanks for pointing that out. Appreciate it. Not."

"Don't worry about the other guy. That's my point. Just focus on building a relationship with Fallon. Unless there's something else you want."

Brandon took a sip of his bottled water and swished it around in his mouth. "What are you getting at, Moore? Just come right out and say it."

Axl put his hands up. "Fine. You want Grace, don't you? Be honest."

That was a tricky question. "If by want, you mean I'm attracted to her, the answer is yes. I mean, it wasn't beer goggles that led me to sleep with her back in the day. I thought she was hot then, and I do now. We had great chemistry. I would love to repeat that but she's already made it clear she'd rip my nuts off if I tried to have sex with her."

"Is that all you want? Sex?"

"You're starting to annoy me," Brandon told him. "Not everyone is going to have some happy ending like you and Leighton." He didn't need to be reminded that this was complicated. He was well aware of that. This wasn't the story where suddenly he and Grace fell in love and got married. Life didn't work like that. Grace wasn't sold on his character and he hadn't been planning to settle down for another five years, maybe more. He had a thriving career that needed tending. Grace and Fallon lived in Minneapolis.

Most of all, you can't force feelings that didn't exist.

"I'm just saying if you don't want her to have a boyfriend, the only way to avoid that is to *become* the boyfriend."

"Are you fucking crazy?" he asked Axl, shocked he would even suggest that. "What, like a fake relationship? That's your deal, not mine."

His friend just shrugged.

Maybe Axl was thinking he'd be like him, and the fake relationship would become real the way Axl's had with Leighton.

That wouldn't happen though.

But Brandon glanced over at Grace and Fallon. Grace turned and gave him a smile, which he returned. His chest felt tight.

Be the boyfriend.

Could he actually do that?

He'd get to know his daughter. He'd get some of his guilt alleviated.

He'd get Grace. In his bed.

His cock went hard at the thought.

It was worth considering.

He stood up and went over to Grace and Fallon. "What do you think?" he asked Fallon, sitting down next to Grace. "Are you having fun?"

She nodded but didn't say anything. She pushed her hair back out of her eyes. "Can I steer?"

"Probably. Why don't you go ask Leighton?"

Fallon stood up and walked over to Leighton, swaying back and forth with exaggeration like the motion of the rocking boat would make her fall. He gave a laugh. "She looks more like a zombie than like waves are knocking her around."

Grace pulled her long legs up onto the seat and crossed them, knocking her knee into his thigh. "Sometimes I think she's a little immature for her age. It's my fault for babying her. I was more independent at her age."

Brandon knew next to nothing about how kids were supposed to behave at what age and to be honest, he didn't remember much about being eight himself. "Were you living with your grandmother at that age?"

She nodded. "Yes. My parents died when I was three. I don't really remember them. My grandmother was strict but she was tired. She had tons of rules but at the same time she made me and my brother fully responsible for ourselves. I was doing my own laundry at five." She wrinkled her nose. "She thought I was pretty soft on Fallon."

He wasn't even sure what the hell to say. So he went with his gut. "I think you're an amazing mother. Look at Fallon. She's happy, she's healthy, she's polite. You should be proud of yourself."

Grace eyed him. "Thanks. You're kind of a nice guy, you know that? You're not living up to my douchebag expectations at all."

That made him laugh. "Sorry to disappoint you. I can do something horrible if you want."

She rolled her eyes. "Like what?"

It was an opening and he decided to walk through it. "Like tell you how sexy I think you are and how I can't stop thinking about kissing you."

Her eyes widened. But at the same time, she leaned almost imperceptibly toward him. "That is horrible."

He nodded slowly. "The worst. Because you don't want me to kiss you."

"No. Not right now."

Grace seemed to realize she had confessed she did want to

kiss him, just not in front of Fallon, because she shook her finger at him and jumped off the bench. "Behave yourself."

"Always."

That made her snort before she went over to check on Fallon. He couldn't help but grin. She wanted him as much as he wanted her.

He made eye contact with Axl. His friend looked bemused.

Be the boyfriend.

Shit.

The idea held a hell of a lot of appeal.

"SHE'S A NATURAL," Leighton told Grace as Fallon held the wheel with a great deal of concentration.

"Thanks for letting her do this," Grace said. "And for letting us crash your day with Axl."

Leighton gave her a warm smile. "It wasn't that long ago I was the outsider here in Beaver Bend. It's hard to jump into a crowd of friends that have known each other for two decades."

Grace sat sideways on the passenger seat and forced herself to remain quiet. Her gut told her to protest, to make it clear that she wasn't jumping into anything, but that would be rude. Leighton was just trying to be nice. It wasn't her fault that Grace was a mess of jumbled thoughts and emotions. "Brandon is lucky to have such good friends. So how do you like living here as opposed to LA?"

Brandon had mentioned Leighton had grown up in Beverly Hills and had met Axl the previous year at the charity event. She couldn't imagine moving from LA to a small town in Northern Minnesota. Then again, she'd never been to LA. Her view of it was the TV version.

"I hate the cold," Leighton said, with a laugh. "But I love everything else about it. People are friendly, the scenery is beautiful, and it's insanely affordable. Plus, of course, I have the love of my life here. What else could I want?"

Leighton did look wildly happy. Grace suddenly envied her with a deep jealousy that caught her off guard. "That's amazing," she said, because that was true and she did appreciate Leighton's happiness. It just made her aware of how truly lonely she was.

She'd had a boyfriend when Fallon was about eighteen months and she had thought they might get married but he had broken up with her after a year, saying he wasn't really ready to do the family thing. Fortunately, Fallon had been too young to be affected too much by the breakup and since then... nothing. Just casual dates here and there. Grace wasn't even sure she'd even been in love with her ex-boyfriend. She had been in love with the idea of being a family, having help, support. He'd been a nice guy, reliable, and kind to her and Fallon and she had thought that meant she was in love. But almost seven years later she wasn't so sure.

She hadn't realized Fallon was even listening until she said, "Mom, who is the love of *your* life?"

Grace answered truthfully, with zero hesitation. "You."

But Fallon wasn't having it. She rolled her eyes, chancing a glance over at them. She was standing with her feet wide apart for balance and she wasn't steering so much as thinking she was steering. Leighton was standing right behind her, one hand on the wheel too.

"Mom."

"What?"

"I can't be the love of your life or your soulmate. That's not how it works. It has to be another adult, not your kid."

"I don't have one. Not everyone does." *Thanks for pointing that out, kiddo.* Grace was part-amused, part-horrified. "People are single. There is absolutely nothing wrong with that and don't let anyone tell you otherwise. We can make ourselves happy."

We can even give ourselves orgasms.

That seemed to have zero impact on Fallon. She gave Grace a sly look. "Maybe it's my dad."

Grace's face went hot. Shit. That was not an idea she wanted Fallon to get attached to because it was ridiculous and was never going to happen. She wasn't Brandon's type if his social media was any indication. Nor was he hers. She wanted someone stable, not a playboy. "I don't think so. If he was, it would have happened a long time ago."

Fallon wrinkled her nose.

Leighton shot her a look of sympathy.

"Time to let Leighton steer again," she told Fallon. "Go sit down by Brandon."

Fallon frowned but Grace didn't care. She didn't like being put on the spot by an eight-year-old and in front of Leighton.

Her daughter dropped her hands abruptly and muttered, "Whatever." She gave Grace some nasty side-eye as she moved past her.

"Hey," Grace said, sharply. "Watch your tone with me."

Fallon gave her a wounded look that made her feel guilty, but she squashed the urge to apologize. Her daughter ran over to Brandon and sat right next to him, like she had done it a thousand times. She even put her hand into his. He looked startled but pleased. He ruffled her hair.

So that's what divorced parents dealt with. Kid gets mad at you, she intentionally tries to make you jealous of the other parent. Charming. Grace felt stunned and more than a little pissed. She reminded herself all of this was a huge adjustment for Fallon and it was going to take time to sort out.

"I wish I had a beer," she told Leighton. "I'm not a big drinker, but the last few days have been intense."

"I have some vodka spritzers in the cooler if you want one," Leighton said. "It's my way of trying to pretend I'm watching my weight."

That made Grace laugh. "I envy your figure," she said. "I've always been built like a thirteen-year-old boy. I don't have a Latin booty at all. I think my Irish grandfather ruined it for me. He was like a reed."

"It's such a woman thing, isn't it? We want what we don't have. But honestly, I've always been cool with being curvy. I just don't want to get any *more* curvy, if that makes sense. Seriously, if you want one of the spritzers, I'll turn the wheel over to Axl and have one with you."

Grace wasn't usually one to drink in front of her daughter, but what the hell. This day wasn't like any other. "That would be great."

"Honey," Leighton called. "Do you want to drive or should I cut the engine and let us drift?"

"Let's drift for a bit," Axl said.

Leighton gave him a thumbs-up and cut the engine.

Suddenly it felt super quiet.

Grace felt at a loss for words. A week ago, she could have never imagined she'd be spending her weekend on a boat up north, the warm sun and the crisp clean air on her.

With her daughter's father.

Despite the circumstances, being outside was very relaxing. She didn't spend much time outside at home. She didn't have a balcony or patio space and she worked mostly at home.

Leighton went over to the cooler and opened it. Before she could return Brandon came up next to Grace. "Fallon's mad at you," he said.

Grace was annoyed. "I figured as much. If we got through today without her being mad at me or you or both of us, that would have been a miracle."

"She wouldn't tell me why she's upset, just that you won't listen to her."

Brandon looked casually handsome in a polo shirt and shorts, sunglasses hiding his eyes. Grace wished that she were no longer attracted to him, but the painful truth was she was incredibly attracted to him. Just like all the other women on his social media.

"She's mad at me because when she suggested that you're the love of my life and my soulmate, I told her I didn't think that was the case. She's trying to play matchmaker, which is something I wasn't anticipating." It honestly had never occurred to her Fallon would suggest they be together.

Brandon didn't look as startled or appalled as he should. "That seems like a normal thing for her to want, doesn't it?"

"Not really. I didn't even know your name until four days ago."

He just shrugged.

Grace couldn't tell what he was thinking. "Well. We need to nip this in the bud. I don't want her disappointed. She's going to have to accept that this is probably the only time you and I will even really interact. Her relationship with you will be separate from what she's always known with me."

Brandon made a noncommittal sound that alarmed Grace.

"Brandon."

"What?"

"We have to nip this in the bud," she repeated.

"Sure. Whatever you want, Grace."

That was not reassuring. She was about to ask him what on earth he was thinking when Leighton returned, handing her a can. "Thanks," she said automatically.

Brandon took the can right back out of her hand.

"What the hell are you doing?" she asked, outraged.

He was popping the tab. He handed it back to her. "Opening it for you."

She eyed him like he had crawled out from under a rock and had three eyes. He might as well. She'd never had a man open an aluminum can for her. "Why?"

"Because it's polite."

"No, it's not. You took it out of my hand. I can open my own can." She wanted to add, *for fuck's sake,* but Fallon might hear her.

"Of course, you can open your own can. That's not the point."

"I don't get you," Grace said, feeling irritated with everything.

"You can open mine," Leighton said, handing her can to Brandon. "I just got my nails done."

Grace had never gotten her nails done. Ever. She wasn't a girly girl to begin with but then she had just considered it an unnecessary expense. It made her want to hide her nails in the pockets of her shorts. Brandon probably dated very polished women. Literally polished. She had been a tomboy as a kid, and she supposed she wasn't much different as an adult. She let her hair do its own thing, she barely wore makeup, and she dressed exactly like she had at eighteen. She owned precisely one dress and it almost never saw the light of day.

Forgetting there was vodka in the drink, she threw her head back and took a massive chug. Then barely managed to prevent herself from spitting it back out. The vodka was subtle, but not when you weren't expecting it and sucked down half the can. Brandon thumped her back, which made her feel less than sexy. Yeah, she wasn't exactly Brandon's type.

He'd gone home with her that night because he'd been drunk and she'd been willing.

That was why he'd given her a fake number.

It was important to remember all of that.

None of this was about her. It was all about Fallon.

"Are you okay?" he asked her.

"I'm totally fine," she lied.

"You're lying," he said. "Try not to worry. Fallon will be okay."

She wanted to scream, "How the hell do you know? You don't know her!" but she restrained herself. He was trying to be supportive. She was grateful he was handling all of this as well as he was. To be honest, he was handling it better than her.

"I'll never forgive myself if this damages Fallon. This is all my fault," she said, taking another baby sip of the vodka spritzer.

"Don't do that to yourself," Leighton said. "You're doing the right thing letting Fallon meet Brandon."

"Thanks, Leighton."

Leighton squeezed her hand, then walked over to her boyfriend.

Brandon put his hands on her shoulders. "Grace. This is my fault. Not yours. Give yourself a break and just try to enjoy this. This is a good thing, right? You don't have to do it all by yourself anymore."

He gave her a smile that warmed her from the inside out even more than the vodka had. "That's going to be a struggle for me, you know that, right?"

With a laugh, he shook her a little. "Since you got territorial about my opening your vodka spritzer, yeah, I figured as much. I know you're superwoman. You absolutely are. But it's okay to accept help."

Grace was a little embarrassed, a little annoyed. Not wanting to make a big deal out of any of this right now, she tried to turn it into a joke. She gave him a weak smile. "It's like you're speaking a foreign language."

"Do you want me to say it in Spanish?" he asked, letting his hands drop off her shoulders.

"Yes." That would put an end to this nonsense.

But then Brandon shocked the hell out of her by telling her she should accept his help, in imperfect, but passable Spanish. She raised her eyebrows. "Wow. I'm impressed. You can tag team with me and teach Fallon. She doesn't seem to have a natural knack for languages. I should have pushed it more when she was little."

"My Spanish is not great. It's mostly conversational, acquired through work the last few years. But I can try." He gave her a grin. "And you just proved my point. See? I can help you."

Damn. He was right. "Bastard," she teased. "You manipulated me."

"Never."

Without warning, Axl started the engine up again. Grace fell forward, colliding with Brandon. He caught her and steadied her. Startled, she murmured, "Thanks," trying to get her footing.

Then she looked up into his blue eyes and she felt like she had lost her footing all over again.

He wanted her. She could see the lust in his eyes.

And admiration.

He *liked* her. Respected her.

It was a reflection back at her of exactly how she felt about him.

Yeah. She was not on sure footing. Not at all.

She had the hots for her baby daddy.

SEVEN

"SO HOW IS EVERYTHING GOING?" Siobhan asked over the phone.

Grace was in her room at Brandon's rental, lounging on the bed and eyeing the hot tub. She wondered how loud the jets were and if she could sneak into it for thirty minutes without Fallon being the wiser. "It's actually going okay. I mean, it could have been a full-blown disaster but so far, so good. Fallon is being a little cranky, but that's to be expected. Right now, she and Brandon are grilling burgers for dinner."

"How domestic. I can't believe you're staying in his house. Isn't that weird?"

It was. But mostly because she was aware of his presence constantly. "A little. But it makes it way easier. Basically, Brandon and Fallon have a week's crash course to get to know each other then it will be an occasional visit here and there, with FaceTime calls in the meantime."

"Is he good with Fallon? I don't know the guy, but I'm picturing him being either inappropriate and dropping F bombs in front of her, or being clueless while she like falls in the lake or whatever."

That had been her assumption as well. "He's neither. He's aware, thinks before he speaks, and he isn't crowding her. He's letting her set the pace."

Grace was lying on her back staring up at the ceiling. She was a ball of anxiety and she wasn't sure why. Everything she was telling Siobhan was the truth. Everything was going better than she had expected. Yet, she was tied up in knots.

"That's awesome, Grace. I guess Jeff Spicoli grew up into a decent guy."

"He did. So, tell me about your hot night with the bar owner last night." She could live vicariously through Siobhan's sex life.

"It was horrible. Just awful." Siobhan actually groaned.

"Oh, no! Why? Erectile dysfunction?" Maybe she didn't want to live vicariously through Siobhan.

"What? Oh, God, no. The opposite, in fact. The man went for like two hours, half of which was going down on me. That's what was awful about it. He's old school. He paid attention to me. He had the oral sex skills no guy in his twenties can ever touch."

Interesting. "So then what's the problem? What is so horrible about great sex?"

"He's ruined my future sex life. No one can compete with that shit. He was fucking nice, Grace. He opened doors and made me breakfast and wasn't awkward or weird or suggest I give him a rim job ten minutes into making out."

Um, wow. "Guys do that? Ask for rim jobs when you've just met?" Maybe she had escaped some horrors while in her self-imposed isolation.

"More than I care to admit. I'm not saying it's off the table forever but let's get to know each other first. That's not for a casual first time together."

"Agree." Vehemently.

"But half the guys I've been with act like going down on me

should get them the Presidential Achievement Award. The act of oral is lost on guys our age. I blame fucking Tinder."

"I can't really weigh in on this. You know I'm basically a nun in denim shorts." Though Brandon hadn't been a slouch in that department all those years ago. He's been generous in that regard. She very clearly remembered that.

"Yeah, well, I might join you after this. I can't go back to two-pump chumps. I just can't. It was like... perfect."

That stunned Grace. Siobhan was never one to sound so soulful or melancholy. She lived life on her terms and bounced from guy to guy whenever a red flag popped up. "Wow. So maybe you should stay in touch with him?"

"I don't think so. He didn't ask for my number or anything. He just gave me a delicious kiss, after driving me to the hotel and walking me all the way to my room, I might add, and thanked me for a lovely night. A lovely night. A lovely fucking night, who says that?"

Apparently, Liam, the fifty-year-old bar owner. "I don't even know what to say other than well, now you have a new standard? Or maybe date older men?"

"I'm miserable," Siobhan said, sounding exactly that. "This sucks."

"I totally understand. I'm pretty miserable too."

"I'm being selfish. My one night of beautiful passion does not compare to the fact that you had teen sex and got pregnant by Jeff Spicoli and now it turns out he is rich and hot."

Huh. "When you put it like that, I'm not sure why either one of us are upset."

"Because these guys are awesome and we can't have them, that's why we're upset!"

"Is it?" Grace wasn't sold on that. Did she want Brandon? Sure, for sex. Which she wasn't going to act on. But for real? Or something more? She didn't think so. They were too different.

He couldn't commit and she was bogged down by responsibility.

"That's totally why we're upset. Trust me. I met a guy that is actually a solid human being who expressed genuine interest in me, and I can't have him. You have a guy you've been vilifying in your mind for nine years and now you find out he's Mr. Awesome. You're imagining a little family unit for the first time ever and knowing you can't have it sucks."

The truth of it hit her like a Black Friday mob at Walmart. Siobhan was right. "I hate you," Grace said, her mouth going hot, though her words held little heat. "Because you're so right it's disgusting."

Ever pragmatic, she had been pretending that she wasn't feeling the same way Fallon was— curious. Wondering what the future could hold. No, she wasn't exactly picturing a happily ever after, but she was... curious. Curious why Brandon hadn't been more appalled at Fallon's suggestion he might be her soulmate. Curious why Brandon looked at her like he wanted to both devour her and worship at her feet. Curious as to what he envisioned his future with Fallon to be.

There was a knock on her door. "Grace?"

Damn it, it was Brandon. "Yes?" she called out. "Siobhan, give me a sec."

"Dinner is ready." Then he opened her door.

"Brandon!" she reprimanded. What if she had been naked, for whatever reason? Geez. "You're supposed to ask before you come in the room."

"Sorry." He didn't look sorry. He looked... hungry. His eyes were raking over her body, from head to toe, pausing at pivotal points along the way.

"Siobhan, I'm going to have to call you back."

"I bet you do," Siobhan said, sounding absolutely gleeful. "Go get yourself some, honey."

"Hush, I'll talk to you later."

She ended the call and started to sit up but the position she was in wasn't that easy to get out of. Her feet were dangling over the end of the mattress and it was either sit up like a vampire or roll onto her side. She started to roll but Brandon moved forward and held out his hand for her. She hesitated, but then took it. She was half-expecting him to climb onto the bed with her, but he didn't.

Because she was an idiot, she was actually disappointed.

He hauled her off the bed easily. Brandon clearly hit the gym. Not that it was shocking news, he had biceps that inspired drooling. But it was good information for the hockey matchup she was determined to have.

"How's your friend?" he asked. "Did she get back okay with Juan?"

"Yes, she did. She also apparently had quite the night with your friend's father."

Brandon shook his head. "Do I even want to know? Did something weird happen between them?"

"No, not at all. She gave him two thumbs up and is now questioning all her previous encounters with men."

He laughed. "Seriously? Wow. I can't wait to rub that in Sullivan's face. Talk about awesome ammo to have on a guy. His dad is a sexual savant."

It had never occurred to her that he would want to give Sullivan shit about it. That was such a guy thing. "Then you're welcome. I'll tell Siobhan you appreciate the information. I'm pretty sure she doesn't have sex for the amusement of others, but she also probably didn't expect me to give you details. I should have kept my mouth shut."

That went to show you how off her game she was. She wasn't usually a blabbermouth.

"I don't know Siobhan but from what I've seen, I'm guessing she wouldn't mind in the slightest."

"Probably not." Grace wondered if Brandon thought Siobhan was hot. He had asked her to dance with him initially, not Grace. Something that felt uncomfortably like jealousy came over her. "In general, Siobhan is more fun than I am."

Brandon reached out and brushed her hair off her face, catching her off guard. She forgot to pull away.

"I think you're a whole lot of fun."

"What are you guys doing?" Fallon said, appearing in the doorway without warning. "Our burgers are going to get cold."

"I was talking to Siobhan. We're coming now," she said, even as she pulled away from Brandon, heat flushing over her face.

God. She was blushing in front of her daughter. That was a new level of ridiculousness. No wonder she didn't date. She acted twelve in front of guys.

Grace shoved her phone in her back pocket and started toward the doorway. Fallon disappeared down the hall into the kitchen, her curls bouncing on her back as she half-walked, half-ran.

Brandon grabbed her hand and stopped her. She looked back at him in question.

"I called my parents. They want to meet Fallon. You let me know if and when."

Her shoulders sank in disappointment. Her heart rate had increased when he'd touched her. She'd thought in that split second that he was going to flirt with her. Or kiss her.

Instead, he was respecting her boundaries with Fallon. Just like she had asked him to.

"Let me think about it. Were they okay with the news?" That had to be a hell of a shock.

"After calling me an idiot every way possible, they were

excited. Disappointed, of course, to have missed so much. Just like I am. But happy."

"That's good. I mean, not that they're disappointed, but that they're happy."

He nodded, but he looked troubled.

"Come *on*," Fallon yelled. "I'm dying of starvation!"

"The kid is hangry," Brandon said. "I can sympathize with that. She must get that from me."

Grace snorted. "Oh, you've never seen me when I'm waiting in a restaurant. I'm like a hissing cat."

Brandon just said, "You don't scare me."

Maybe not. But she was scaring herself.

BRANDON WAS EXHAUSTED. He had spent the last five hours trying to get Fallon to say anything of substance to him but she wasn't having it. She'd eaten dinner then had wanted to go back down to the lake. He'd taken her for a walk through the woods and had tried to discuss her hobbies, school, friends, but she had blown him off for the most part. She had asked for a bonfire when the sun had gone down and he had complied but then she hadn't sat still, mostly poking at the logs with a long stick until Grace had reprimanded her.

He knew it was unrealistic to think that Fallon would be all cozy with him but she had a lot of energy and he wasn't used to catering to a kid. He hadn't been this tired after a night of debauchery in Vegas where he hadn't gone to bed until the sun was coming up. At least this was a good tired, as he sat on the deck sipping a bourbon, instead of the wrecked kind. But at the same time, it just illuminated the fact that he had no fucking clue what he was doing when it came to being a parent.

Was the day a success? He had no idea.

Was Fallon okay with him or did she think he was a complete tool? It was anyone's guess.

He wanted to press Grace on her thoughts and opinions but at the same time he didn't want to put anything more on her than he already had.

He wasn't used to not being able to control a situation or solve it with logic. As a kid, he'd been intrigued by people who ran their own businesses and knew he'd never be the guy to work for someone else if he could avoid it. He'd become his own boss where every decision was his, for the most part.

That was how he liked it. Being in charge.

This wasn't his element and he had essentially no power.

He had to let Grace call the shots.

She looked as exhausted as he felt. She was wearing pajama shorts and a tank top with no bra, which was destroying the little peace of mind he had left. He could clearly see her nipples through the tight fabric. She was in the lounge chair next to him with her eyes closed, though she wasn't sleeping.

Fallon was in her room, and he hoped she was actually asleep, and not going to pop out from behind a slider.

"Can I get you anything?" he asked Grace. "Do you want a glass of wine?"

"No, thanks. I just want eight hours of sleep but I know if I go lay down I won't be able to sleep. My mind is racing." She opened her eyes and looked at him. "Your kid was on crack today."

That made him laugh. "Oh, now she's my kid? Nice try. I think she's just... processing. Right? Or is she always like this?"

"She has a lot of energy, but not like this. I think she doesn't know what to do with her emotions."

"That makes two of us."

"Three of us," Grace added.

"What do we do now?" he asked. "You tell me. Is this too

much? Should we ease up? I can go stay with my parents if you think that makes more sense." He didn't want to but he didn't want to overload Fallon.

"Did we scare you off?" Grace asked with a small smile.

"No, not at all. I just want to do what's best for Fallon and not be selfish. This is all your call. I'm just spitballing ideas here."

"I don't know. Maybe we are muddying the water and confusing her. Maybe now that she knows you a little bit, you can take her to your parents for a few days and I'll just stay here on standby in case it goes south."

The thought terrified him. One, because he didn't feel qualified to be alone with Fallon. Two, because he didn't want to leave Grace here by herself. It all seemed wrong.

"Are you sure she wouldn't freak out on me?" he asked dubiously.

Grace blew out a breath. "Honestly, she might. It's probably not a good idea given that she's really only ever stayed with my grandmother or my brother." She groaned. "Oh my God, what are we even doing?"

He knew what they *should* be doing. It involved him drawing her nipple into his mouth through that tank top and slipping his hand up under her pajama shorts. He stood up and came behind her and put his hands on her shoulders. He started to knead the knots she had in her tense muscles.

She moaned in a way that turned him on. "That feels good. I'm really tense."

"It's a lot. But we both need to find a way to relax. Maybe our nerves are rubbing off on Fallon, I don't know. I don't claim to know anything but I do know you feel like you have pretzels in your shoulders."

Grace's head dipped forward, hair tumbling onto her chest

and baring her neck. He wanted to kiss that beautiful length of skin.

"I don't know how to relax," she said.

Brandon ran his thumbs up the back of her neck, massaging her gently, but firmly enough to elicit another moan from her. He didn't have any sort of formal training, but one of his indulgences was twice monthly massages and he'd picked up a trick or two. "Let me help you relax."

"I don't know if I can. I'm worried. Aren't you worried?"

He was a lot of things. Worried wasn't necessarily one of them. "No. Things have a way of working out in the end. I'm not worried so much as I'm feeling intense. Diligent. Like I'm watching every move Fallon makes."

"That's the same thing as being worried," Grace said dryly, rolling her head as his hands shifted back down to her shoulders.

That surprised him. "No, it's not. Being worried means you're stressing out without taking any course of action. Most situations and problems have a solution or at least a way to manipulate them."

"Easy for the rich guy to say. Try being a single mom working her ass off to make sure the lights don't get shut off all while knowing your kid will never go to science camp or take vacations to Caribbean resorts."

Brandon shifted a wavy strand off of Grace's neck so he didn't accidentally pull it. Her words didn't upset him or make him feel defensive. She was speaking the truth. "You're right. Except I wasn't born with money. I'm not some trust fund baby jet-setting. I work my ass off too, but for me, the reward has been financially greater than it has been for you. On the flip side, you've raised a happy, intelligent child. It's apples to oranges."

Grace sighed. "I liked you better when you were just the douchebag who gave me a fake name."

That made him laugh. "What? Why?"

"Because then I could just be angry with you and dismiss you. Now I... can't."

Her words warmed him. They also turned him on. "Then maybe you stop trying."

She glanced up at him over her shoulder. "What does that mean?"

"How about I just show you." He was playing with fucking fire, he knew it.

But he didn't care.

What he cared about was Grace. With a depth that surprised the hell out of him after a mere twenty-four hours. She was an amazing woman who impressed him on every level. He wanted more than just the polite arrangement of a barely there father to his child's mother. He wanted friendship with her. Passion. Maybe something even more.

He moved to the side of her lounge chair and reached for her hand. "Stand up."

"No. I'm tired."

Grace sounded like Fallon had earlier when she'd been told she couldn't have any more potato chips. Just a little bit bratty. Yet for some reason it was completely sexy. Because he knew that she was being petulant because she was struggling to resist and that was hot. She wanted him as much as he wanted her.

"Fine." Brandon sat down on the chair, easing her legs over a little first. He turned so that he was facing her and cupped her cheeks, the way he had that night they'd met. Out in the snow. "You're so beautiful," he said. He ran a thumb over her bottom lip. "I'm going to kiss you. Now is your chance to say no."

He expected her to shoot him down. Grace had spent too many years being responsible. Her worry would supersede any desire for him.

But Grace surprised him. She just lifted her chin and said,

"Do you remember that night? You said the exact same thing. Is that your standard line?"

He shook his head. "No. I just wanted to give you a chance to push me away. Then and now. I remember way more from that night than you think I do."

"What do you remember?" she murmured, even as her eyes drifted down to his mouth.

More than he should, given how loaded he had been. "I remember dancing like an idiot, then turning and this girl with legs a mile long smiled at me. And I walked over to you and I asked you if you wanted a drink and you said yes. It was a rum and Coke. I sucked your lime when you finished it."

Her dark eyes went soft, and filled with desire. "Wow. I'm impressed."

"Then we went outside so I could bum a smoke off the doorman, doing that smoking-while-drinking thing, but once we stepped outside and I saw you in the moonlight, snow drifting down on us, I forgot about anything but kissing you."

He even remembered what they had talked about then. She had talked about sled dogs and her desire to ride on a sled behind a team.

"You need to shut up and kiss me," Grace said, her hands reaching out and splaying across his chest. "Before I either change my mind or I do something really stupid."

Part of him wanted to ask what that something stupid might be. The smarter part of him realized he might lose the opportunity to taste her lips if he questioned her further.

"I can do that." He leaned further into her and covered her mouth with his.

He intended it to be soft, exploratory. A sweet kiss. A kiss to acknowledge what they shared together— a child.

It was instantly more than that. The second his lips touched Grace, everything shifted between them. Chemistry had been there nine years ago. The burbling spring of youthful passion. This was a volcano that had been waiting to explode.

This wasn't about polite co-parenting.

This was about what they started as drunk and reckless kids.

She wrapped her arms around his neck, making a delicious sound of surrender.

Grace tasted perfect, her kisses hot and demanding.

Brandon shifted closer, wanting all of her. He teased at her lips with his tongue, demanding she open for him, while his hand drifted down to brush over her tank top, finding her nipple.

But instantly she stiffened and pulled her head back. She was breathing hard, eyes wide with desire and fear. She dropped her hands to his chest, as if to hold him at bay.

"This isn't a good idea. I'm a mom, I have to put Fallon first."

"Yes, but who is Grace? Doesn't she have needs?" Brandon took her hands and pulled them down between them, holding them tightly so she wouldn't try to run away from him. He tried to meet her gaze, but her gaze had drifted away to somewhere over his shoulder at the woods.

Grace was biting her bottom lip and she sighed.

Finally, she locked eyes with him. "Grace got left back somewhere at the University of Minneapolis in a twin bed in a dorm room. Now I'm just a mom and a woman who does her eight-plus hours a day for a paycheck."

He hated that. Everything about that. He suspected Grace wasn't naturally that person, who just settled into drudgery. "Fallon is older now. I'm going to give you child support. There is time for you now, Grace."

She shook her head and tried to pull her hands away. "Uh, stop. I don't want you to feel sorry for me. That's not the fucking point. I don't feel sorry for me. I don't regret my life, Brandon. I don't have this rousing social life, so what? It's all good. In another few years Fallon won't want me around at all."

He believed her. But at the same time, he believed she wanted more. "I don't see why you have to wait another five years to do that. Maybe it's finally time for you to rediscover who you are."

He half expected her to cuss him out. That seemed her style. He knew he was responsible for a lot of the hardship Grace had endured and he was absolutely overreaching here. He knew it. But it was partly his guilt spurring him on. Grace deserved to have some fun, even if it really wasn't any of his damn business.

Grace made a sound of impatience. "I think you've mistaken me for someone who likes to talk about my feelings."

That made him laugh. "Okay. Then no talking. Just take what you want."

"You know what I want?" she asked, cheeks flushed and eyes fiery with passion. "I want orgasms. That's what I want. I'm sick of providing my own."

Holy fuck...

Brandon had never heard anything sexier in his entire life. "I can do that."

EIGHT

GRACE HADN'T IMAGINED herself telling Brandon she wanted an orgasm, but she was frustrated. She did not want Brandon feeling sorry for her. He had been looking at her all day like she was this martyr to motherhood and she wasn't.

Not dating was a choice. Being a mother didn't mean she couldn't, she just chose not to in order to make life easier. She had no opinion on other women who did date. To each her own, she firmly believed that. For her, not dating had just made reality less complicated.

She didn't really miss being in a relationship. But she did miss sex.

"What are you going to do?" she demanded, crossing her arms over her chest. It was a defensive posture, she knew that, and she absolutely hated herself for throwing a challenge out there, then needing to shield herself.

"I'm going to give you an orgasm."

She believed he could. She wanted him to. If he had been capable of the feat at twenty-one when she'd been drunk, there was no telling what heights of ecstasy he could drive her to older with her sober. But she needed to make one thing clear. "I'm not having sex with you. I'm not getting pregnant again."

He gave a half-laugh. "Fuck, that would be the ultimate irony, wouldn't it?"

"It's not funny!" She was in her bedroom and she glanced back at the hallway, fearful they were being too loud. "I don't need to tempt fate."

"There is seriously no way that would happen twice. Besides, I have condoms."

"Of course you do." He probably bought them in bulk. "But you did nine years ago too." She was using an exaggerated whisper, trying to keep her voice down.

"That was different."

"How?" she asked, well aware that he was moving closer and closer into her personal space. His hand had suddenly appeared on her hip. "Same penis, same me! How is it any different?"

Brandon looked away, rubbing his jaw, and she could tell he was trying not to laugh.

She smacked his chest. "I'm serious, don't laugh."

"It's kind of funny, you have to admit." His fingers started to shift from her hip to the front of her waist. "By the way, why do you get to be you and I'm reduced to a penis? Shouldn't it be same penis, same pussy?"

She was a little shocked. Mostly turned on. "I think technically it would be penis and vagina. Or cock and pussy. Don't you?"

He nodded, while popping open the button on her denim shorts. "I think you're right. I should never doubt that you're right."

"Now you're starting to figure this whole thing out. Repeat after me: Grace is always right."

To her shock, he did it.

"Grace is always right. Happy? And you saying cock is a huge fucking turn-on, but you know that already, don't you? You said it just for that reason."

"Oh, I said it to be right. But turning you on is a side benefit." She may be out of the game but she still remembered how to play.

"So, you really don't think we should have sex?" he murmured, his hand running down the zipper of her shorts, making her want to groan.

"Same kids, same sandbox," she said. "It's not a good idea."

"Oh, come on." Brandon kissed the corner of her mouth. "What's the worst that can happen? We give Fallon a little brother or sister."

She reared back and smacked him again. "What is *wrong* with you?" She realized immediately by his expression he was joking.

"I'm kidding." He put his hands out to block any further attacks. "I'm totally kidding. I solemnly swear not to get you pregnant."

"I want that in writing."

"I'll get my lawyer on it." He held his hand out to her. "Now come into the bedroom with me or I'll go down on you out here."

Grace shivered. Instantly, her body responded to his words. She was wet, her nipples beading, a groan escaping. But while she was horny, she wasn't stupid. This deck might be facing woods but behind it was an entire wall of glass. There would be absolutely no way to hide anything if Fallon decided she was weirded out in a big house and wandered out of her room to find her mother.

Meaning, not only did they need to go into a bedroom, they needed to lock the door behind them.

She took his hand and let him pull her to her feet. "This is probably the second dumbest thing I've done in my adult life."

"I guess I don't have to ask what the first was. But what's dumb about getting what you deserve?" Brandon reached out and cupped her cheek. "Let me make you feel good, Grace."

Her thoughts were racing but her body didn't give a shit. She was absolutely going to let Brandon make her feel good. Her justification was it was actually less complicated than it would be to date. This had no strings attached. They shared a daughter, but they weren't in love and never would be. She knew they had chemistry. No one was going to get hurt or emotional. It was the perfect way to scratch her itch.

"I have no objections to that," she told him. "So I guess that means I get to go first."

He laughed. "Of course. Ladies always go first." Brandon opened the slider that went to her bedroom and they went inside the cool bedroom.

He pulled the door shut behind them and locked it. Clearly, he understood the risk involved. He went to close the blinds while Grace moved to the hallway door and pushed in the button to lock that as well. She didn't feel nervous. Just a little rusty. She was comfortable around Brandon, despite the oddity of their circumstances.

So instead of being a shy eighteen-year-old waiting for him to take the lead, Grace kicked off her sandals and peeled her tank top off. She dropped it onto the chair by the stairs to the hot tub. Before she returned to Minneapolis she wanted to use that hot tub. Preferably with Brandon in it with her.

"Need some help?" Brandon asked when she reached for the waistband of her shorts.

That amused her. "I'm pretty sure I can handle it on my own, but thanks."

"You're missing the point." He came over and flicked his

finger over the strings on her cotton shorts. He pulled the waistband out a little. "Letting me help would be more fun. Less... utilitarian."

Grace paused. He had a point. "You mean, the goal isn't to be as efficient as possible?" she joked. "I have a busy parent's mentality. Get in, get out."

"Since you won't even let me get in, I'm sure in the hell not going to rush through this."

He teased over the swell of her small breasts, making her shiver.

"Unless you've changed your mind about that." He brushed his hand over her nipple as he spoke.

She was more amused than annoyed. "Nice try, but no. Don't ask again or there will be consequences."

His eyebrows shot up. "Mom voice. Damn. I'm not sure if I'm scared or turned on."

Grace smiled, mischievously. "You should be both."

Brandon's light eyes narrowed and he gave a low growl. "Fuck, you are so hot."

Then he bent over and took her nipple into his mouth. Grace shivered, feeling the pull of his warm touch all the way deep inside her. He teased at her with his tongue, taking his time, thoroughly working her over until she was digging her nails into his shoulders and panting, wondering how something so simple could feel so damn good.

"Remember we have to be quiet," she said, which was apropos of nothing. Brandon wasn't making any sound at all. Maybe she was worried about her own ability to stay silent.

"Of course," he said, before moving to her other nipple and taking his time there as well.

For years she had been ignoring her sexual needs, or at least downplaying. Which wasn't easy when she had to watch porn for work. But she'd managed to convince herself that she didn't need sex with a man. She'd been lying to herself.

She was burning from the inside out just from the sensation of Brandon's wet tongue swirling over her nipple. Her panties were damp and he'd barely touched her.

When he pulled back and murmured, "Get on the bed, Grace," she eagerly complied.

She sat down and shifted herself backwards on her elbows. Brandon watched her, his nostrils flaring a little. She briefly wondered how many women he had been with, then told herself none of that mattered. This was fun, nothing more.

He climbed on the bed, pausing to pull his shirt off, before putting a knee on either side of hers. She couldn't say she really remembered what his body had looked like nine years earlier, but she did know for sure he was much more muscular now. He was a man, not a boy. She reached out and ran her touch over that firm, warm skin of his chest. She wanted to explore and because of their brief history and their shared child, she felt an odd sense of right to intimacy that she wouldn't have with another man. She didn't know Brandon well, but it seemed the nature of their relationship allowed her privileges it wouldn't have with someone else.

Brandon seemed to feel the same way. He pinched her nipple, lightly, teasingly and said, "You're pretty fucking hot, you know that, right?"

"Feel free to tell me that whenever you want," she said. "I promise not to get a big head."

He gave a soft laugh and twisted her nipple just a little harder.

"Oh, damn," she said and gave a startled moan. Then she clamped her lips shut. "Shit, was that loud?"

"Not at all." Brandon undid her shorts and slipped them down over her hips.

Grace kicked them off, wanting to be totally naked and free to feel all of Brandon over her. She put her hands on the waistband of her panties, determined to ditch them, but he stopped her.

"What's the hurry?"

Was he joking? "I haven't had sex with a man in probably eighteen months. That's the hurry."

"Which is why we shouldn't rush this."

He had a point. "I hate it when you're right."

Brandon grinned. "I know you do."

Before she could respond he had dropped his head down and kissed her clit, through the fabric of her panties. She threw her head back and swore under her breath. This was going to be delicious torture.

Especially given that he abandoned her clit after barely brushing over it and shifted so that he could kiss her. "Let's make out," he said. "Like we did that night."

This was how she'd gotten pregnant the first time. There was something so sweet in his seduction. It made it very hard to say no to him.

For that reason, she wrapped her arms around Brandon's neck and kissed him old school. Like she was eighteen and all those physical desires could be stirred just from mouth on mouth, stroking, gliding, tasting. It made her feel lighter, reminded her of a time before responsibility ruled her life.

They kissed and kissed until their breathing deepened and her lips felt swollen and she had an ache so deep and intense she couldn't stop her hips from rising and pressing against Brandon. He had a thick erection and she wanted him inside her so damn bad.

She cursed the fact that they wouldn't be able to have sex. She wanted to, to just allow him to ease into her with a single thrust, and stroke her to completion, but she was too scared of consequences.

Brandon finally, after what felt like hours of sweet torture, slipped his hand inside her panties and eased over her swollen and aching clit. Then he sank a finger inside her wet channel. Grace gasped, amazed at how good that felt.

"I want to taste you," he said, and took her panties down to her knees. Gripping her thighs, Brandon shifted her legs apart.

The first touch of his tongue on her sensitive clit nearly sent her through the roof. She'd been celibate too long and it was intensely stimulating.

"You like that?" he asked, massaging her with his fingers at the same time he blew cool air over her.

"Yes," she breathed. "Though I'm not sure how long I'm going to last."

Brandon didn't respond with words. Instead, he buried his tongue inside her and stroked with a deft touch that had her moaning way louder than she had intended. She clamped her hand over her mouth so she wouldn't wake up Fallon in the next room.

"Oh, God," she whispered, arching her hips to meet more of his mouth.

It had been far too long and he was far too skilled.

She didn't want it to end too soon but it felt so deliciously good she knew it was going to if she didn't stop him. After enjoying a few minutes of his attention, she pushed his head away.

"What's wrong?"

"It's too much," she said. "I'm too close. Let me suck your cock for a minute."

Brandon paused in the act of wiping his bottom lip. His eyebrows shot up. "Like I'm going to say no to that."

She started to sit up but he pushed her back down. "Just stay there. Nice and relaxed."

He took his shorts down and brought his erection to her. Grace gripped his shaft firmly with her right hand and flicked her tongue over the tip. She wanted to take him, to taste him. She was so insanely turned on she wanted to drive him as crazy as he made her. She felt a little wild, a little free. Even though she was acutely aware they weren't alone and that they couldn't have sex, she still felt more like Grace, the woman, than Grace, the mother.

She eased her lips over him and took him fully into her mouth.

Brandon gave a sharp hiss and gripped her head with his hands. "That's it. So fucking good."

He was easy to read. When she did something he liked, he gripped harder, and thrust into her. She loved the validation that she was arousing him, driving him closer and closer to explosion. Running her fingers over his balls, she took him deep, opening her throat.

Brandon swore. "Grace."

She pulled away and looked up at him in the dark room. "Yes?"

"Sit up."

"Why?"

"Because I'm going to come."

She wasn't sure what his point was but she enjoyed the urgency in his voice and the way he just about dragged her to a sitting position. He teased the tip of his cock over her lips in a blatant request for more and she took over, excited by how hard he was.

It only took a few strokes before he was there, giving a deep low moan as he emptied his pleasure into her mouth.

Grace thought it was the hottest thing ever and she kept sucking until he pulled back.

She barely had time to swallow before he pushed her back down. Then he bent over her and ate her pussy with a steady, intense rhythm. Given how excited she was, it was barely a blink before she was biting her lip, closing her eyes, and letting the wave of ecstasy crash over her.

It was like flying. She let go of everything. Her worries, her fears, her yoke of responsibility. She shattered and enjoyed the impact, holding on to Brandon with both hands.

She was wide-eyed and breathing hard and wondering what the hell had just happened when Brandon rolled over and pulled his shorts up. He looked like a bull about to charge.

"Grace, that was so damn sexy that I have to kiss you right now and leave before I try to get you to change your mind." He brushed her hair back, his nostrils flaring. "I want to sink inside you so bad. Damn it. So, I'm saying goodnight and getting the hell out of here."

She nodded, knowing that was probably the best thing to do, even if she didn't want him to leave.

Brandon gave a kiss, then groaned and pulled himself off the bed. "I'll let myself out the back way."

Grace finally found her voice. "Goodnight, and thank you."

He gave a soft laugh and shook his head, retrieving his T-shirt from the floor. "My pleasure." He paused like he was going to say something else but then he just left out through the sliding door to the deck.

A minute later she heard him moving down the interior hallway to his room.

Fingers still trembling she climbed out of bed, found pjs in her suitcase, and got dressed, acutely aware of her body and how fantastic Brandon had made her feel.

The irony wasn't lost on her that the first man to ring her

bell so thoroughly in years was the man she had spent years hating.

It was that night in college all over again.

She had the best of intentions until he smiled at her.

Then she was nothing but a mass of hormones.

But... she didn't regret then.

And she sure in the hell didn't regret now.

She slept better that night than she had in years.

BRANDON WAS SIPPING his coffee and pulling the eggs out of the fridge when Grace wandered into the kitchen. "Good morning," he said, giving her a smile.

"Hi."

Grace's cheeks turned pink and he knew she was thinking about the night before. So was he. Hell, it was all he could think about. She had been amazing, breaking so easily for him. He knew she was underserved in that capacity. He was looking forward to giving her many more orgasms.

She had put on a bra this morning, which sucked. He'd preferred her natural look the night before when she had clearly been too exhausted to have her guard up.

But she looked better today, so he couldn't complain. She looked relaxed. Her caramel-colored hair was tousled and enticing. He wanted to run his hands through it and tug.

"How did you sleep?" he asked.

"Better than I would have expected. I think certain distractions helped." She gave him a grin.

"Same here." He really wanted to kiss her. He glanced toward the hallway to the bedrooms. "Is Fallon up?"

"No. She's the only kid I know this age who can sleep half the day. Put her in a dark room with air-conditioning and she'll lay there like a piece of veal."

He laughed. "Wow. There's a visual. Do you want some coffee?"

"I'd love some."

He reached up for a mug and started to lift the coffeepot out to pour but Grace was instantly there, pushing him out of the way.

"I can pour my own coffee. You don't have to do that."

But he wasn't going to relinquish the handle. "I know you can. But I want to do this teeny tiny little thing as a nice gesture so let me, Grace. Let me do nice things for you."

She wrinkled her nose. "Why?"

Damn, she was stubborn. "Well, because it's polite for a host to make his houseguest feel comfortable. Because you're the mother of my child." He leaned in close to her and murmured in her ear. "Because you sucked my cock last night. A little coffee isn't much after that."

Grace shivered. "I did do that, didn't I?" She licked her lips, like the memory excited her.

He nodded. "Oh, yes, you very much did and it was hot as hell."

"Fine, pour me coffee." She backed up a little. "No touching during the day. That still stands."

He knew that was the way this needed to go down. Fallon was confused enough. They couldn't be overly intimate around her and mess with her head. "But at night?"

"At night, I'm hoping you'll do all kinds of touching."

"But no actual sex?" He understood her reticence. But he figured with a condom that had to be akin to getting struck by lightning twice. It happened, but the odds weren't great. Nonetheless, he would respect whatever parameters Grace wanted to put into place. He was getting more than he had ever expected. He would take whatever intimacies she was offering.

"I thought I told you if you asked again there would be consequences."

"Oh, just try to punish me," he told her with a grin. "I'll turn the tables on you so fast you'll be screaming 'spank me harder' before you know it."

Grace laughed. She took the coffee mug he handed to her and sipped. "That will never happen. Ever."

He loved a challenge. It's what made him great in the corporate world. He also knew that eventually she would cave and he could sink his cock inside her. Again. Sober this time. The anticipation was exhilarating. "Never say never, Grace. You should know that."

She rolled her eyes, something she did frequently. "So, what's on tap for today?"

"Do you want cream or sugar?" he asked, eyeing the way she just drank her coffee black like that was normal.

"No. I always drink it black."

"That makes no sense," he told her. "People who love themselves use creamer." Granted, he used too much, but he figured since he didn't add sugar it all balanced out.

Grace snorted. "Do you know how much sugar is in creamer? That just means you like sugar, not coffee. I actually like the taste of coffee."

"Why does that not surprise me? You're a badass in all things, is what you're telling me."

"Yep." She shot him a grin. "Especially in hockey."

"You're not going to drop that, are you?" Brandon took a sip of his own creamy, sugar-filled and delicious coffee and opened the carton of eggs. He pulled out a frying pan. "I'll have to see when we can get into the rink."

"What are you doing?" Grace asked, her expression one of horror.

He looked at her blankly. "Making breakfast. Are you vegan?"

"Of course not, I ate a steak last night."

"Oh, right. So why are you looking at me like that?"

She pursed her lips then said, "Nothing. I just feel weird having you wait on me."

There it was again. She was not used to anyone doing things for her. Hell, just being nice. It wasn't anything crazy. "It's eggs, not a five-course meal. Anyway, you asked me what we're doing today. The answer is whatever you want. I'm here to please." He cut a hole in two pieces of bread and put them in the frying pan.

"I don't know what there is to do around here. I'm sure Fallon would be fine just hiking or swimming. I guess I can take her to get a swimsuit. I should probably do a little work."

Brandon cracked an egg and dropped it into the bread hole. "You don't know how to spend a day doing nothing, do you?"

Grace leaned against the countertop, coffee mug in her hands. It was covering her mouth. Her luscious decadent mouth that had been wrapped around his cock... damn, he wanted her. All of her.

"I don't think I do." She gave a shrug. "I think I'm broken."

He laughed. "You're not broken. You just need to learn how to transition to the next phase of your life. You've been in survival mode for a long time."

"That's true. Okay, so what is this next phase, oh, wise one? Are you applying to be my life coach, by the way? Because I think I just like you giving me orgasms better."

"Cute. No, I'm not trying to be your life coach. But I think we should call this 'Grace Gets Hers.' That's the next phase." He cracked the second egg and dropped it in the pan. He couldn't undo the past but he was serious about helping Grace going forward.

"I don't even know what that means. I already told you I don't want your money."

"That's not negotiable. If I'm going to have any visitation at all, you're getting child support. That's the way the system works." He turned the burner off and looked at her, lifting his own coffee for a sip. "I'm not going to argue with you about it. Use the back support to do whatever you want. Buy a new car or go on a cruise with your friends or make a down payment on a house. Get yours. That's what I mean."

He was a firm believer in a reward system. He worked hard, but he played hard too. There had to be balance and Grace had never had that. It hadn't been in her reach and now it could be.

"That's ridiculous. I don't need to spend money just to spend money. I don't need a new car. And I'm not going on a cruise. Fallon can't stay with Juan for a week. He's not that patient."

Brandon raised his eyebrows. "Or... she could stay with me."

"In a year maybe, sure. But not now."

"Fair enough. But I think you're missing the point."

She opened up the cabinets one at a time until she found the plates. She took two down and set them on the counter. "I'm in a good mood because I'm still sexually satisfied from last night, and I'm feeling like we're going to do okay with this whole situation overall. For those reasons, I'm not going to tell you to stop giving me advice on how to live my life and shove your money up your ass."

Her smile was sweet and her tone was mild, but he knew there was fire behind those words. He needed to back off. "I'm glad to hear it, and now that I've said what I want to, I'll keep my mouth shut from here on out, I promise. I don't want to piss you off." Even if he was thinking about her best interests. "Though I do want to keep you perpetually sexually satisfied."

Grace leaned around him and poked the egg. Her hip

brushed against his. When she turned to him she put the tip of her finger that had touched the food into her mouth and sucked it. "Eggs are ready."

Brandon dropped his hand onto her narrow hip and drew her to him. "Kiss me."

"We're in the kitchen."

"I'm aware of that." He kissed the side of her mouth, then buried his head in her neck to place kisses on her clavicle.

Grace pushed him away, which he had expected. "I'm not getting busted. Stop it."

"Please?" He gave her his most charming, devil-may-care smile. "Just one kiss?"

"Has any woman ever said no to you?" she asked, looking both bemused and annoyed. "Maybe I'm the woman to knock you down a peg."

"Maybe you are." He needed that. He had reached that point in his life where if he were ever going to get serious about a woman and settle down, it had to be someone who stood up to him, who called him out on his shit.

Axl had told him to be the boyfriend. But that wouldn't work with the situation he and Grace had. It couldn't be just dating, or just seeing where it could go. It had to be all or nothing, because of Fallon. Be the boyfriend? He couldn't picture it.

For years he'd been choosing to date women who worshiped or idolized him because hell, who didn't want an ego stroke? It gave him the upper hand, which may or may not make him a dick. He hadn't studied it too closely. He just knew it was easy and fun. But if he were ever going to get married, have a family, that wasn't the right woman for him.

It was a woman like Grace.

Be the husband. Be the father. That's what he could be with Grace and Fallon.

The thought was like a bucket of ice water over his head.

He took a step back. "The eggs are going to get cold."

His heart was racing and he felt like he did when he made a huge, risky business decision. Adrenaline pumped through him, thoughts tumbled, accessing pros and cons and return on investment. Weighing the risk against the potential payout.

He always studied facts. Then in the end his gut played a huge part in any corporate decisions he made.

Right now, facts were telling him what the hell made more sense than a real relationship with Grace? He hadn't been thinking he would settle down just yet, but hell, they had a kid and chemistry off the charts. On paper, it looked damn good. He could give Grace and Fallon the life they deserved and gain access to his daughter full-time. He could hear Grace making those soft sounds of pleasure every night.

His gut wasn't so sure. His gut thought he was an idiot to give up the bachelor life with a woman he didn't really know.

His gut also told him Grace would tell him to go fuck himself.

Time to gather more facts. He plated the egg-in-a-hole for both of them and set them down at the kitchen island.

Grace sat down and took a bite. "Don't quit your day job. These are overdone." She gave him a wink.

Fucked. That's what he was. He was so completely fucked.

NINE

SUNDAY AFTERNOON, Grace was determined not to fan girl over Jesse Lambert but she didn't think she was succeeding given the pissed-off look on Brandon's face. She just couldn't believe she was lacing up skates two feet away from a pro hockey player who had been team MVP two seasons in a row.

"That goal you had in the last twenty seconds of the playoff game last year was just... wow," she told Jesse. "Amazing."

"Thanks." He was sitting on the bench next to her lacing up his own boots. "Some days you wake up feeling like a winner."

Brandon snorted. He was ready to skate, stick loosely in his hand in front of them. "That is such an asshole thing to say."

Grace was too starstruck to think any such thing. "Hush, Brandon."

Now he really pulled a sour face. "No," he said sullenly.

It was like dealing with Fallon. She couldn't help but want to get in a little dig at him. Apparently, Grace the former daredevil who liked to give it as good as she got, still had a little mischief in her. She gave him a soothing look. "It's okay to be jealous, that's a normal feeling, but that's no reason to downplay someone else's accomplishments."

Jesse cracked a laugh.

Brandon shook his head. "You're lucky you're a mother, because sometimes, Grace, you're as annoying as my guy friends, but with a female spin on it. You start off sounding like it's going to be nice, then you slice with the precision of a hibachi chef."

"That's what I was aiming for," she said, giving him a sweet smile. "And don't think of me as a mom on the ice. I want a fair game."

He held his hand out to help her to her feet. "Not a chance. I'm going to go easy on you."

"I wouldn't underestimate her," Jesse said, standing up. "She seems like the type who might surprise you."

That made Grace feel a little giddy, no lie. "Thanks, Jesse," she said, and she blushed. She felt the heat, which was embarrassing, because Brandon saw it too. He squeezed her hand, and it felt more possessive than tender.

If he had looked sour before, he looked furious now. She had to admit, it was satisfying to see that he was jealous. He didn't like her crushing on Jesse. She tried to pull her hand out of his but he held on to her tight.

"Grace is a buck fifteen," Brandon told Jesse. "There is no way physically she can beat me. That's not an insult, just reality." He pulled her up against his chest. "Pretty, but skinny."

If Fallon wasn't in a public place she would have kneed him in the nuts. That's precisely what she would have done to her brother.

But she wasn't seventeen anymore and Fallon was at the rink with them. She was currently at the snack bar with Brandon's friends Rick and Sloane and Rick's little sister, River, who was a couple of years older than Fallon. Normally, she wouldn't feel comfortable letting Fallon run around a public place on her own, but Brandon trusted his friends to keep an eye on her, so she trusted that. That was something about small-town life that was entirely foreign to her. Everyone seemed to know everyone.

Sloane and Rick had both been very open and friendly to her and no one seemed to think it was anything other than awesome that she was allowing Brandon and Fallon to get to know each other as father and daughter.

Fallon had seemed excited to have another girl to hang out with for a few hours. They both came running over as Grace extracted herself from Brandon's hold.

"Are you sure you don't want to skate?" Brandon asked Fallon.

Fallon made a face. "No! I hate ice-skating." But then she seemed to realize she might dent her new friendship. "Unless you want to," she said to River. "Because then I can, I guess."

But River was clearly in Fallon's anti-sports camp. "No way. This girl does not do ice skates. I excel at academics, not athletics."

Brandon had warned her River was an old woman trapped in a child's body and Grace now understood what he meant. "We'll be right on the ice," she told Fallon. "If you need anything just let me know. Stay with River and her brother and sister-in-law."

"I know," Fallon said, sipping her slushie and looking embarrassed. "I'm fine, Mom."

Grace turned and headed to the ice. She slowed her steps when she heard Fallon say, "Parents are so annoying."

She mentally eye-rolled her daughter suddenly trying to be cool to impress the older girl.

"Don't worry about it," River replied. "At least your mom cares. My parents are whatever. My dad has been married three times and my mom has been to rehab like seven times."

"I never knew my dad's name until yesterday," Fallon said,

like it was a competition. She actually sounded proud of the fact.

Grace glanced at Brandon to see if he had heard. He shrugged.

"Hell if I know," he said. "If you're going to ask me what we do or say to that."

She sighed. "No. I'm just going to roll with it. No worrying. I swear. Though she might need counseling after all of this is over."

"Probably. But look at River. She's normal for the most part, and we're way more pulled together than her parents."

"That's reassuring," she said dryly.

She stepped onto the ice with the rental stick Brandon had gotten for her. She wished she had her own skates because these felt overly worn and misshapen, but she had sold her skates after Fallon was born. Maybe that's what she needed to do when she got home. Find a way to fit hockey back into her life. Because after a few tentative strokes, she fell right back into the rhythm of skating.

She was wearing padding over her jeans and shoulder pads. She adjusted her helmet and wondered if this was smart to do without a mouth guard. Too late to worry about it though. It was just a friendly skate. Brandon didn't look worried at all. He only had on knee pads and a helmet.

Grace skated backwards, just to get the feel again. It was exhilarating, the speed, the freedom. Brandon had dropped a puck on the ice and she skated up and played with it, shifting it around and around with her stick, reacquainting herself.

Then she took a shot at the goal. It hit the back of the net and she grinned in satisfaction. Granted, there was no goalie, but it still felt damn good. The sharp thwack of stick on puck was a sensation she hadn't even realized she'd missed until right now.

"Nice shot," Jesse said, skating past her.

She giggled. She didn't mean to. But her legitimately favorite player was five feet away from her, telling her she'd made a good shot, and treating her like part of his friend group. It was everything. So, she giggled for the first time in probably a decade. Or maybe since the night Fallon had been conceived. She was pretty sure she had giggled in delight over Brandon's flirting.

"Thanks, Jesse," she said with a smile.

Brandon came to a stop next to her as Jesse went center ice. "He's a manwhore," he said, tone annoyed. "With a big ego. Don't make it any bigger."

"I'm not doing anything," she said, embarrassed he had noticed her reaction to Jesse's compliment. "And it's my understanding you're a manwhore too, so I'm not sure why you're telling me that."

"One, I am not a manwhore. Two, I'm telling you that he's flirting with you and I hate it."

That made her roll her eyes. At least Brandon was honest. "He is not flirting with me. Relax."

Jesse was being friendly and nothing more. He was in front of the goal.

"Try another shot," Jesse called out to her. "I'll goaltend. Show me what you've got."

That was nerve wracking but a challenge she was not about to back down from. "I'm rusty," she warned. "But I'm also fast." She looked at Brandon. "Try to block me."

Jesse laughed. "Brandon's slow so this should be easy for you."

"Funny, asshole," Brandon called loudly.

"Brandon!" Grace shot him a look of disapproval. "That was kind of loud. No swearing in front of Fallon, please."

He didn't answer. He just stole the puck from her and took off.

"Oh, really?" Grace said, skating after him. "Not that easy, Blackwell."

He was grinning, looking pleased with himself. "What do ya got, Grace? Show me your stuff."

She shook her head and cocked a hip. "You're going to regret egging me on."

"I doubt that."

She charged him, slamming straight into his shoulder with hers, knocking him off balance so that she could steal the puck back out from under him.

It took him completely off guard. He did manage to recover his balance but by then she was moving down the ice. He cut her off ten feet from the net so she changed direction and headed toward the wall to go around the back and take a side shot. She was focused on losing him, loving the challenge of trying to control the puck while maneuvering toward the goal. She'd forgotten how exhilarating it could be to play the game.

When Brandon tried to retrieve the puck from her again, she was having none of it. She body checked him straight into the wall. Brandon slammed into the glass hard and she took off, taking a shot at the goal. Jesse blocked it but it was still a good effort. If he wasn't a professional player, she probably would have gotten a goal.

"Dang it!" she called out but she wasn't disappointed. She was having a blast.

"That was an amazing block," Jesse said. "You smoked Blackwell."

Brandon didn't look upset as he came over to her. He was actually shaking his head and giving her a grin. "I stand corrected, Grace. You are a lot tougher than you look."

"Bro, I think she's exactly what your ego needs," Jesse said.

"Did I hurt you?" she asked, as sweetly as she could.

"Not at all." Brandon leaned in and gave her that look, the one that made her pants fall off. "I find it hot as hell."

"Besting you on the ice turns me on too," she told him.

Brandon laughed. "You're something else. I can't wait to get you naked."

"Is it bedtime yet?" She glanced over at the stands and saw Fallon sitting there with River, now eating popcorn, and looking perfectly content.

"I wish," Brandon said.

Fallon waved to her. She waved back.

It made her heart full to see Fallon enjoying herself.

There hadn't been enough free time in the last few years for her to give Fallon a lot of fun activities like this. Grace worked a lot of hours and money had always been tight. Their apartment was in a residential area, but there wasn't a park close by, and Fallon wasn't a city-girl. This small town was right up her alley.

It was too bad Brandon didn't actually live in Beaver Bend. Fallon would love visiting him here.

It was like Brandon read her mind. "Fallon seems to like it here," he said. "She seems to have hit it off with River."

"She's handling all of this really well." Part of her was holding her breath for the other shoe to drop and Fallon to have a meltdown, but aside from some attitude and immature comments, Fallon was doing really well. "It probably helps that we're being nice to each other."

"I'm sure it does." Brandon reached out and flipped the end of her hair. "I can be really, really nice to you."

She wanted him to kiss her. She knew she couldn't let him, but she couldn't prevent herself from leaning forward just a little, her eyes dropping to his mouth.

Brandon shifted so that he was closer to her, his left hand going to her waist.

Then he gave her a little push so she slipped backwards.

And he stole the puck from her.

That made her laugh. She went after him. "You're going to regret that, mother*pucker*."

Brandon laughed too and they ended up crashing into each other again, sticks grappling for domination. Grace was breathless and happy and having fun.

Jesse skated past them. "Get a room. There are children present."

"We're not doing anything," Brandon protested.

"No, but you've managed to turn this into foreplay."

They had. They were both trying to dominate, and the air between them was sexually charged. Grace caught Brandon's eye and the laughter died on his lips. The look he gave her was so raw, so filled with lust that it took her breath away.

She slid her tongue over her bottom lip to moisten it. "You can't beat me," she murmured. "Just so you know your efforts will go to waste. I'm very stubborn."

"I know you are. I don't care what the end result is. I like playing with you." He winked at her and shifted backward. "Want a slushie?"

"Always."

The moment between them was gone. Whatever the hell it had been. Grace felt oddly disappointed but it was for the best. They were in public and she had no idea what they were actually doing.

Other than each other, that is.

"I thought you'd never ask," she said, lightly.

Ten minutes later she was sitting with Sloane, while Fallon and River played a video game, and Brandon was on the ice with Jesse and Rick. Her muscles were already stiff from her earlier skating and she realized she was more out of the game than she cared to admit.

"So how do you like Beaver Bend?" Sloane asked. "I lived in Minneapolis for a few years and coming back here was a mixed bag. Lots of pros but a few cons."

"I've never lived in a small town," she said. "I think I would like it. It's cool that everyone knows everyone. I don't think I know a single person in my apartment building's name. It's kind of sad."

"That is true, everyone definitely knows everyone. And everything. Like the fact that I know your friend hooked up with my father."

Oh, right. That. Grace made a face. "Geez. Um, sorry?"

Sloane laughed. "Don't apologize. My father is clearly a grown man and can do what he wants. I just don't want to know about it. Yet I've had like six people tell me about it already." She shrugged, pushing her dark hair back off her shoulder. "Not that my father would be the one over-sharing. He's a steel trap. But that's my point. Small towns can be gossipy."

"Are you trying to tell me something?" Grace asked, genuinely curious. "Is there gossip going around that I should know about?"

"Oh, no! I didn't mean that. Seriously. It's just different here, and my husband embraces it. He won't ever go anywhere else. But Brandon seems happier in the city."

Grace still felt like Sloane was hinting at something but she had no idea what. "Brandon seems happy anywhere with sunshine and lots of bikini-clad women."

She was joking, but it sounded sharper than she intended. She realized she was jealous of those bikini-clad women.

The thought was horrifying.

She had never been the type of woman to carry a purse or wear false eyelashes or perfect the art of walking in heels. It had never bothered her. She was who she was and she was totally fine with being something of a tomboy.

So why the hell would she care if Brandon vacationed with a bevy of supermodels?

She watched him skating, all broad shoulders and dark hair. He was more graceful on the ice than Rick and she thought he was insanely good-looking.

Grace wanted him for herself.

That's why she was jealous.

She had gone and done the unthinkable.

In one weekend, she had fallen for her baby daddy.

Maybe she'd never gotten over him in the first place.

"Brandon has had fun with those girls. But maybe what Brandon needs now is a woman who can give it right back to him." Sloane gave her a long look. "A woman like you."

Grace waved her hand in dismissal even as her throat felt like she'd swallowed a peach pit. "I'm here for my daughter and nothing else."

Except an orgasm or two.

That night Grace locked her bedroom door and avoided Brandon's hints and flirtations. She couldn't shatter beneath his tongue knowing she was stupid enough to actually like him.

She lay in bed, ankles crossed, body aching for his touch, reminding herself that he had given her a fake number nine years ago.

There was no way she should or could fall in love with a man like Brandon.

His grin danced behind her closed eyelids.

She groaned and rolled onto her stomach.

Which just made her pussy ache even more.

Her phone buzzed.

It was a text from Brandon.

A kiss emoji.

She stared at it, her finger slipping inside her panties.

Stroking herself, she thought about his tongue teasing at her clit. She rocked her hips onto her finger, realizing there was something completely insane about touching herself to thoughts of him touching her all to avoid having him come in and touch her.

Grace came, face buried in her pillow as she gave a soft cry.

She rolled onto her back. It was official. She was a hot mess.

TEN

STANDING on stage stripping and finding out he had a daughter was by far the number one most shocking moment of his entire life.

Walking in to Grace's room and finding her sitting at the desk watching porn was right behind it.

He had knocked to let her know the quick pasta and salad dinner he had made was ready, but she hadn't answered. He had thought she might have fallen asleep, or better yet, was in the hot tub, so he'd opened the door.

Nope. She was not resting her eyes or soaking away the day's tension.

She had on headphones, was sitting on the chair with her legs crossed, and staring at the screen, where a very muscular man was enthusiastically sliding his cock in and out of a woman's ass. The woman had huge breasts and a look of pure pleasure on her face. Acting or not, Brandon bought it. A good time was clearly being had by all. He wasn't unaffected, especially given the fact that Grace had been dodging him the last few days.

Now here she was, casually typing while watching pretty

basic, but pretty right-up-in-their-business porn, and he had an instant hard-on.

He tapped her shoulder.

Grace jumped and the movement made the headphones pull out of the computer. The sound of moaning filled the room. Then the guy slapped the woman's ass and the crack of his hand on her skin made Brandon jealous, he wasn't going to lie. Brandon felt blue-balled and this guy was getting some, big-time.

"Oh, geez, you scared the shit out of me," Grace said, looking around him as she dropped the headphones to around her neck. "I thought you were Fallon. That's my biggest fear, that she'll catch me doing this. I thought I locked the door. I always lock the door."

"You must be out of your routine. Dinner is ready." He looked at the screen again. "I don't get it. What the hell are you closed captioning? 'Oh, baby, harder,' over and over?"

"Pretty much. But I'm also supposed to convey the tone of their voice. So I put things like, 'Mike aggressively tells Angel, I'm going to tap that juicy ass.' You know, stuff like that." Grace's cheeks turned pink as she shrugged. "It pays the bills."

Brandon reached over and hit the sound button on her laptop. "I can't concentrate when there are sex sounds coming from the computer. Do you... get turned on?" he asked, because he was very curious about that.

What turned Grace on? Did she have a vibrator in her desk drawer for when work got a little hotter than usual? There was an image he couldn't shake. Grace, legs up on the desk, a buzzing buddy being eased inside her.

Damn it. He adjusted his cock inside his jeans.

Grace glanced at his crotch. "Clearly you do."

"What can I say? I'm picturing you turned on and touching yourself."

She hit the pause button on the video. Unfortunately, it was right at a close up of penetration. Brandon raised his eyebrows. She frowned and slapped her lid shut. "It's a job, Brandon. To be honest, most of it is boring. Tab A into Slot B kind of thing."

He was a little disappointed, but he could see her point. "It probably looks fake, huh?"

She nodded. "Except there is one actor in particular. I'm really fond of his work. He has a magnificent cock and I just love the way he seduces the women."

Magnificent cock. What the fuck? His blood started to boil.

Grace started laughing. "Your face. I'm dying."

His shoulder relaxed. "So, you're yanking my chain? I guess I deserve that."

"Yes," she told him. "And yes, sometimes I do get turned-on. I don't get out much so despite the redundant nature of it, sure, it can be a turn on. But if I really want to get hot, I prefer a book or a sensual movie, where the sexual tension builds so that when they finally get together it's a big wow."

Brandon was standing behind her and he started to rub her shoulders. "So, you want a buildup, huh? You're a secret romantic for all your tough girl words."

"I'm not a secret anything," she said, glancing back at him. "What you see is what you get."

"I like what I see." He brushed her hair back as he gently massaged the muscles in her shoulders. Then he bent down and kissed the soft flesh of her neck. "I'd like to see more of it."

"It's six p.m. Go away."

Sometimes she made him feel like a kid who got caught with his hand in the cookie jar. He pulled a face and dropped his arms. "Fine. But dinner is ready if you're hungry. And my parents are on their way."

With that, he moved out of her range, fast. If he knew

Grace, she was capable of whacking him for not telling her earlier.

"What?" Grace's hand went to her hair and she tried to smooth it down. She opened her laptop again and started clicking around, like she was saving her work. The video in the right corner was still just a closeup of some random guy's dick. "How soon will they be here?"

"Twenty minutes. I asked if they could stop by tonight and you said yes."

"I thought you meant like *later*." She dropped her headphones on the desk and bit her lip. "This is going to be awkward."

"Are you kidding? We've got the market cornered on awkward. I told you my name was Jeff Spicoli. You told me we have an eight-year-old child while I was on stage stripping at a charity event. We're talking about my parents with some guy's junk on your computer. We could write a manual on awkward."

"Don't be a drama queen."

Brandon laughed. "You're the one who said it's going to be awkward."

"Then you took it next level." She smiled at him. "Now let me change my clothes before we eat."

"Can I watch?"

"Oh, wow, you are just... twelve."

"If you think ninety percent of men, regardless of their age, wouldn't have said that or at least be thinking it, you are dead wrong. I'm just saying. Besides, you never know unless you ask."

Grace crossed her arms over her chest. She looked more amused with him than angry, but she pointed to the door. "Go."

"Fine." He went toward the door. "Do you want any wine?" He turned and nearly swallowed his tongue.

Grace was standing in her underwear.

He made a strangled sound in the back of his throat. "That's dirty pool, Martinez."

She bent over her suitcase. Bent. Over.

He saw a whole lot of tight ass.

"I'm being efficient. Remember? That's my thing."

"Yeah," he said dryly. "I remember. Get your pants on before we have to delay dinner while I eat you instead."

She didn't look worried. She just smiled at him. "You're so cute."

Grace was infuriating. She was also sexy. Hilarious.

And besting him at whatever game they'd been playing all week.

It only made him more determined than ever to win.

GRACE ACCEPTED the hug from Brandon's parents as best she could. She wasn't much of a hugger and she felt awkward embracing total strangers. But she did it because she was grateful that they were interested in Fallon and clearly determined to make things as normal as possible.

The Blackwells were nice and natural with Fallon and they weren't crowding her. They had introduced themselves and had briefly hugged her, but didn't push a further conversation.

"So, tell us about yourself, Grace," Mrs. Blackwell, who had asked her to call her Susan, said.

Brandon had suggested everyone sit out on the deck, which allowed Fallon to draw with chalk on the wood boards. It gave their daughter the ability to separate herself if she needed to. Fallon didn't necessarily have drawing talent but she had a brilliant imagination. Or at least to Grace she did. She might be biased.

"Hm, me? Let's see. I do closed captioning in Spanish." She refused to look at Brandon. She hadn't been totally truthful with him earlier. Porn or not, she was in a constant state of arousal since she'd arrived in Beaver Bend, and it was all his fault.

She should have never given in on that first orgasm. Now it was all she could think about and she needed to stay strong so she didn't lose her heart. But damn, it was hard, getting harder by the minute.

And now she was thinking about having sex with him while his parents were politely trying to get to know her. Ugh.

"I have a brother, Juan, who just got married. His wife is very sweet and I'm very happy for them. I love hockey but honestly, I don't have much time for hobbies. I work two jobs."

Brandon's mother had the kind of polish Grace never would. She was elegant and beautiful, with shoulder-length hair she'd let go gray, but had added a violet wash to. She had on a flowing kimono and skinny jeans and jewelry that was interesting but not overly matching. His father, Ben, was the same way. Casually sophisticated, with salt-and-pepper hair. It was easy to see where Brandon got his charm, confidence, and taste from. While it made Grace feel more than a little working class, it didn't bother her. She was proud of who she was and how hard she had worked to provide for Fallon. That didn't mean she really knew what to say about her life though. What the hell was she supposed to say?

"I'm very impressed with what you've been able to accomplish," Susan said, and it sounded genuine to Grace. "I'm hoping now that we all are aware of the situation we can help you out. We really appreciate you allowing us the opportunity to get to know Fallon."

"I'm happy too," she said sincerely. "I don't have much family. Just my brother. I want Fallon to have family she can count on."

"She absolutely does," Ben said. "And so do you, Grace. You're family now too."

For some reason that made her throat tighten and she felt the sensation of tears rising. Embarrassed she just nodded and looked over at Brandon, feeling panicked. He was sitting in the chair next to her and he put his hand on the back of her neck and massaged the knots beneath her skin, trying to reassure her. The panic passed but she still had no idea what to say.

Fortunately, Susan seemed to sense that. She pulled an envelope out of her purse. "After Brandon showed us a picture of Fallon, I was amazed at how much she looks like him as a little boy. I brought some pictures so you can see what I'm talking about."

Brandon groaned. "Mom, are you serious? You brought baby pictures of me?"

"I want to see!" Fallon jumped off the deck and came running over. She sat on the bottom of Susan's chaise, clearly comfortable with the Blackwells.

"Here's one," Susan said, pulling it out and handing it to Fallon. "This is your dad in first grade at Christmas when he got a scooter. Look at how silly his hair was here. He insisted on that Mohawk."

Fallon laughed. "Wow. You're so little, Dad."

"Let me see that." Brandon held his hand out and Fallon gave him the photo. "Hey, I was pretty cute. What do you think, Grace?"

He showed it to her. "You're adorable," she said, and she meant it. He was a cute kid. Fallon definitely had a lot of his features. "Nice toothless smile."

"Here you are with the boys on the hockey team." Susan handed Brandon another picture.

He grinned. "I think I was about thirteen here. Crazy. These guys are like brothers to me." He showed it to Grace. "There's Axl, Jesse, Sullivan... and believe it or not that short, round kid is Rick."

"That's Rick?" Grace was stunned. "Puberty definitely helped his cause." He bore no resemblance in that photo to the muscular man he was now. Sloane had told her Rick had crushed on her in high school but she had thought of him as a friend only back then. It was clear to see why in this picture. He looked five years younger than the other guys.

"We used to call him Little Dickie. He hated that nickname."

"Let me see," Fallon demanded. "That's River's brother?" she asked, sounding as incredulous as Grace felt.

"Yep."

"So, do you like being an only child, Fallon?" Susan asked. "Brandon sure loved it."

Fallon shrugged. "I don't know. I guess. I mean, a sister would be cool."

Grace wasn't sure where that question came from but Fallon didn't seem bothered by it.

Brandon cleared his throat though and gave a slight head-shake. "Mom."

Susan looked chastised. "Sorry. I just meant it as conversation."

Fallon was flipping through the stack of photos in Susan's hand. "I feel like this is what I would look like as a boy. Hey, Dad, let's face swap. Mom, let me have your phone."

Grace obligingly handed over her phone after opening the app Fallon wanted. "Here you go."

Her daughter went over to Brandon and sat on his lap. He wrapped his arms around her. Grace's heart almost burst at the sight of it. It was something she had never, ever thought she'd be able to give Fallon. She could have sworn she actually felt her ovaries flutter.

They made goofy faces at the screen then both laughed out loud when they saw the swap.

"Let me see," Grace said.

Fallon turned the phone and showed her. Brandon looked like a man wearing a wig with Fallon's curls on him. And Fallon looked odd to her with the short haircut but it was very clear they were father and daughter. Their features weren't that different from one another. "Brandon, you look good with long hair," she teased.

"Sure, if I ever want to join a grunge band."

Fallon showed Susan and Ben who both looked amused, and a little shell shocked. "Good Lord, there is no doubt, is there?" Susan said.

Grace knew they meant Brandon's paternity.

"It's a good thing I actually gave birth to her," Grace joked. "It doesn't look like she got any of my genetics at all."

"She got your brains," Brandon said.

More like her stubbornness, but she was not about to admit that. "She didn't get my daredevil side, thank God."

"Well, hopefully she got your strength and your compassion," Susan said.

Grace felt it again. Her heart squeeze.

Her whole life she had wanted a bigger family, and then the same for Fallon.

It looked like Fallon had found one if she wanted it. Grace was grateful at the same time she felt... lonely. For the first time, it occurred to her she might end up alone at some point. Fallon would grow up and then what? The idea of never getting married had never bothered her before. She had a pang or two at the thought of never having any more children, but she had enough time still she didn't think about it often.

The good part about finding Brandon was that if something happened to her, there would be someone else besides just Juan to help Fallon through life. She had a father and grandparents to join her uncle. Even if nothing happened to her and she lived to be ninety Fallon was going to want to spend time with Brandon and his parents.

Where did this new reality leave her?

Alone.

Maybe that was why she was afraid to let Brandon in.

He wasn't offering her a future but that's precisely what she wanted. A husband. A family. More children.

"Thank you," she told Susan, even though too much time had passed to be strictly polite.

"No, thank you for giving us such a gift." The sun was setting over the lake and Susan put her hand up to block it, smiling at Grace.

The view was spectacular, the sky all pinks and purples, the lake rippling.

But that wasn't the view that was holding her awe and attention.

Grace watched Brandon and Fallon taking more selfies, this time giving each other rabbit ears.

This was why she couldn't have Brandon touch her anymore.

Suddenly the idea of Brandon knocking her up again was far too tempting.

ELEVEN

BRANDON HANDED Fallon a popsicle and ruffled her curly hair. Each day that passed it sank in further and deeper that she was his daughter. His flesh and blood. It was strange how quickly and totally his life had changed and how grateful he was for that.

When he looked at Fallon, he felt awe. Pride. A fierce protectiveness.

He felt love.

He had already learned to love her in less than a week of having her in his life and it was profound and beautiful and amazing.

She seemed, if not quite as enamored of him as he was of her, graciously tolerant.

Her mother was a different story entirely. Grace was avoiding him at night and he had no clue why. He couldn't pinpoint what had gone wrong. At the hockey rink, he'd been convinced she had every intention of letting him in her bedroom again that night. Instead, she had claimed she had to work. At ten o'clock at night.

Every day since had been the same and while he absolutely

loved having Fallon with him he wished he knew what her mother was thinking.

"Thanks," Fallon said, ripping the wrapper off the popsicle and handing it back to him.

He wanted to tell her there was a wastebasket two feet away in Rick and Sloane's kitchen, but he figured he hadn't earned that right yet. Which she clearly knew, because she was playing him. He strongly suspected she wouldn't hand a wrapper to Grace. But he was willing to let it ride for now.

"You're welcome. Now go outside so that thing doesn't melt all over the floor."

Fallon gave him a thumbs-up and ran out the back door of the kitchen into the massive yard. She was having a blast at Sloane's birthday party playing with River and the family dog. Brandon swiped an olive off an antipasto tray and popped it into his mouth. Sloane was getting a water from the refrigerator.

"Do you need any help?" he asked her.

"I'm good, thanks." She closed the fridge and smiled. "I'm glad you could be here. We don't see you often aside from when you're in town to strip."

He rolled his eyes. "Funny. I guess it has been awhile since I've been back in the Bend. I can't believe what you and Rick have done with this place. It looks nothing like it did when we were kids."

Sloane and Rick had bought her and Sullivan's childhood home from their father, who had decided he was done with keeping up with a big house. It had a huge yard that was mostly untouched but inside Sloane had traded all the nineties oak for a modern farmhouse vibe. There wasn't a wallpaper border in sight.

"I felt kind of guilty changing out the décor," she said, glancing around like her father might pop up and overhear her. "But we had to make it our own home. It's not like it was my dad's style anyway. My mom picked everything out, then skipped town so hey, if she was all about looking forward, I figured I could do the same thing."

"Well, the house looks great so good job."

"You ever think about buying a house?" she asked.

It was kind of an odd question but Brandon just shrugged. "I don't know. Condo life suits me for now."

"What about Fallon?"

Brandon looked out through the patio doors. He could see Fallon eating her popsicle and petting Sloane's dog, who was patiently waiting for the popsicle to fall off the stick. Sloane's father, Liam, and Sullivan were out there too, along with Sloane's aunt and some of Rick and Sloane's friends. Winnie, who owned the groomer's, was there, along with Axl and Leighton. Grace was sitting with Leighton and they seemed to be having a good conversation, both smiling.

Grace and Leighton seemed like polar opposites, Leighton being what Brandon would call a girly girl. But they'd hit it off on Axl's boat and seemed to be fast friends now. Maybe because they were both outsiders to Beaver Bend.

"What about Fallon?" he asked, unable to drag his gaze off of Grace.

Every day they had spent together, he had grown to admire and respect her even more. She handled everything with strength and calm, including meeting his parents. Every single thing Grace did, she thought about her daughter first and the impact on her. Brandon couldn't have asked for a better mother for his child than Grace.

"I know that River has thrived since we moved here to the house, with the yard. Grace told me Fallon loves being outdoors."

Brandon had never thought of Sloane as being interfering. Mostly as a kid he remembered her as Sullivan's big sister, chronically annoyed with all of them. She hadn't been interested in her brother's pack of rowdy guy friends at all. But apparently, marriage and home ownership had her thinking everyone needed a life of domestic bliss.

"I think Grace knows what's best for Fallon, not me." That wasn't his role and most likely never would be. He had to defer to Grace's opinion on everything regarding Fallon.

"Unless the two of you get together." Sloane gave him a grin. "Just saying."

Considering Grace wouldn't even let him touch her anymore, he didn't see that happening. Brandon shook his head. First Axl, now Sloane? Apparently, all of his friends wanted him to make an honest woman of Grace. "When did you become a matchmaker? And speaking of kids, when is Rick going to knock you up? You're not getting any younger."

"Shut up, I'm only thirty-two." But then Sloane gave him a sly smile. "He already has. I'm ten weeks. Sullivan and my dad know but we haven't told River yet."

He didn't consider himself a sentimental guy but the news that his teasing was in fact, true, and his friends were starting a family, fucking choked him up a little. Rick and Sloane had known each other for twenty-five years and now they were having a baby. Damn. Life was clipping along.

"Seriously?" He reached out and gave her a hug. "Congratulations, then. I'm really happy for you both. Happy Birthday, Sloane."

She hugged him back and swiped at her eyes. "Thanks. Now go drink a beer for me since I can't."

"I can do that."

He started for the door.

"Just think about it, Brandon. You could have a really great future."

What he wasn't about to admit was that he had considered

what was next. That he had thought about Grace with another man and had hated the idea. At the same time, he'd thought about her with him and he'd been very intrigued by that idea. But he didn't know how to convince Grace that he was willing to change his entire life for her and Fallon. She wouldn't believe him.

Hell, he wasn't even sure he believed himself. It was risky as fuck and Fallon could get really hurt if they screwed up.

Maybe Grace was right to avoid him.

"I think about a lot of things," he told Sloane. "Including my daughter."

"Sometimes you end up right where you started. Like me and Rick."

He shook his head, amused. "Someone has been searching quotes on Pinterest."

"Jerk."

"But charming and rich." He shot her a grin and went outside.

GRACE WAS HAVING such a great time in Beaver Bend she realized she was dreading the return home to her cramped apartment. Brandon was driving her and Fallon back to Minneapolis in two days because school was starting in two weeks and Grace needed to get back to work. She was squeezing in work time, but this little impromptu semi-vacation in the country had to end.

She was going to miss the fresh air, the view of the woods from the rental house, the smell of the lake, and the extra time spent with her daughter. Not to mention she wasn't looking forward to not seeing Brandon anymore. She liked his company. He was funny and thoughtful and well, hot. Even if she had been resisting the urge to have sex with him, she had still enjoyed being around him.

Now a whole week had gone by and they had settled into a routine. Brandon worked for a few hours in the morning while she hung out with Fallon, then in the afternoon she worked and he had time alone with his daughter. Then they ate dinner together and sat out on the deck watching the sunset.

It was a routine she was enjoying. Too much.

"Can we have a dog?" Fallon asked. She was clearly in love with Kate, Sloane's dog.

"No, I'm sorry, sweetie. You know our apartment doesn't allow pets and it wouldn't be fair to a dog anyway. They need a yard."

"Can we have a dog here?" she asked Brandon, not missing a beat.

Grace knew her well enough to know that had probably been Fallon's plan, to ask Brandon, knowing full well Grace would tell her no.

"I don't usually live here," he said. "I have a condo in Chicago and it's not dog friendly."

"What? You don't live here? That *sucks*. So I can't come back here?"

Grace was sure they had told Fallon the house was a rental but that was a week ago and information had been coming at her fast and furious. She'd met her father, grandparents she'd never known she had, and had made a friend. She'd been swimming and hiking and fishing and having the absolute time of her life. Brandon's parents had been super sweet to Fallon and had taken her horseback riding.

"Well, probably at some point to see my parents, if it's okay with your mom. But mostly when you want to stay with me, it will be in Chicago."

"But I like it here, not Chicago."

Fallon was loving life in Beaver Bend.

Grace had a crazy thought pop into her head.

Why couldn't she and Fallon move to Beaver Bend?

If Brandon gave her the money he was saying he was going to, she could probably afford a condo or a small ranch house. With a real yard for Fallon to play in. An easier, slower lifestyle.

Grace could work anywhere, so that wasn't an issue.

It was definitely something to think further about. Maybe a little nuts, given she'd only been in town for a week but once the idea took hold, she couldn't shake it.

Brandon didn't live there, so it wasn't like she would make things awkward with him.

She used to be the girl who followed her heart. Who took a leap of faith, who went for what she felt passionate about.

Maybe it was time for that again.

"I'm sorry, Fallon," Brandon said, looking guilty. "I have a business in Chicago. If it's okay with your mom, I promise we can come here at least once every summer."

Fallon didn't answer. She just held out her empty popsicle stick to Kate, who licked it enthusiastically. Then she handed the stick to Brandon and said, "Come on, Kate." They both went running across the lawn.

Brandon rubbed his forehead. "I feel bad. I know she loves animals. Maybe I should buy a house in Chicago. What do you think?"

She was touched. "I think you should only buy a house if you want to and feel like you can take care of it. Otherwise, you'll just resent having to deal with it."

Her words seemed to piss him off. "Don't tell me how I would feel, Grace."

Her eyebrows shot up. "That's not what I meant."

"I think it is. I think you have this idea about my life that isn't true. I'm not really a party guy. Most of my adulthood has been spent building a business. Then I take one or two vacations a year."

She wasn't sure what he was getting at. "You're clearly very successful. You should be proud of yourself."

"I am. But I don't seek success so I can splash money around and get women. I do it because I like a challenge and I like to push myself."

"Why are you angry with me?" she asked.

"Because you're putting words in my mouth. And you're avoiding me. What changed from the other night? You wanted me, I wanted you, and we had a great time."

Grace glanced around, hoping like hell no one was listening to this conversation. The only person within earshot was Liam O'Toole and he looked like a man who had no opinions on how other people lived their lives.

"I don't know if this is the time to talk about it," she hedged.

Brandon gave her a deep, searching stare. "Then tonight. Don't shut me out."

Hadn't she just vowed to be more open, more willing to take a leap into the unknown?

She had no idea what Brandon wanted from her or if he just meant sex but either way she wanted to know.

Giving him a nod, she said, "Sure. Of course." Then because she was determined to be herself, and recapture some of her zest for life, she added, "Though I have to warn you I was planning to try out that hot tub tonight since we're leaving in two days."

He gave a scoff, like he couldn't believe her audacity. "Damn it, you're going to kill me. Is that an invitation to join you? Because if it is, I'm in. And if it's not, you're a cruel woman."

No, she wasn't cruel. She was a woman who had spent the past few days trying to protect her heart. Now she realized there was no way to do that. The second she had thought Brandon was well and truly upset with her, her heart had sunk anyway. He was right. They needed to talk. She couldn't save her feelings by shutting him out.

"It's an invitation," she said. Then she couldn't help but tease him. "You said we should talk and I agree. What's more relaxing for a serious conversation than a hot tub?"

"I take it back. Not cruel. Evil. You're just evil."

Then he reached out and took her hand, lacing her fingers through his.

She let him, because it felt good and right.

Because she was falling in love with him.

TWELVE

FALLON LET Brandon accompany her to bed that night. She insisted she was too old to be tucked in, but he could turn the light out for her. It was good enough for him. Hell, he was just grateful she didn't hate him. Anything beyond that was a gift.

She jumped on the bed and crawled toward the pillows. "I wish this was your house," she said, glancing toward the woods. Moonlight streamed in through the wall of windows.

He kind of wished it was his house too. He wanted to give her everything he hadn't up to now because he had been a twenty-one-year-old fuckup. "It's cool, huh? I'm glad we got to hang out here together."

"Yeah." Fallon turned back and looked up at him. "Are you going to blow me and Mom off after this trip? River said her parents are always blowing her off."

Brandon had a lot of opinions about River's parents, none of which were appropriate to share with Fallon. He settled for, "No, I promise you I will never blow you off."

"You'll visit me at home?"

He nodded, his throat tight. "Yes." Shit, maybe instead of

Chicago he needed to buy a house in Minneapolis. That way he could spend a couple of weekends a month there with Fallon. He really dug spending time with this quirky little girl. She was pretty amazing.

Especially when she shocked him by sitting up and wrapping her arms around his neck and laying her head on his shoulder. "I'm glad I got to meet you," she said.

Holy fuck, his heart. It damn near exploded in his chest. "Me too. I love you, Fallon." He did, with a fierceness that belied the length of time he'd known her, but felt nothing short of life-changing.

"I love you, too, Dad."

She'd asked to call him Dad and she had already done so a couple of times. It almost killed him every time. Nothing that had happened in his life prior to now was as important as this moment where she was well and truly accepting their relationship. He kissed the top of her head, taking in the scent of her shampoo from her shower. "Goodnight, kiddo."

"Night." Fallon fell back onto her pillow. "Are you sure we can't stay here longer?"

"That's not for me to decide. Your mom is the boss. We both have to listen to her always, you understand me?"

Fallon made a face but nodded.

Brandon stood up and clicked off her lamp. "See you in the morning."

"Yepper depper."

That made him smile in the dark room. Fallon was a great kid.

Grace was in the kitchen pouring herself a glass of wine.

Brandon was so overcome by emotion he had to stop at the end of the hallway to gather himself. She didn't see him, so he watched her for a minute as she hummed a song and did some goofy little dance move to whatever music was playing in her head. He had to ask himself why he remembered as much as he did about the night they'd met and conceived Fallon. He really shouldn't. He had been loaded. The night should be mostly a blur, but all his time with Grace was sharp and clear. Why was that?

And why when he looked at her now, did he think he was in love with her?

They had chemistry, even though she was holding him at arm's length. Then and now.

She was smart, she was savvy, she was responsible, stubborn, loyal. She could dish out crap and she could take it. She was a savage on the ice.

He was in love with her.

He listened to his gut. It had never failed him before.

"Grace."

She looked up and smiled at him. "Hey. Everything okay? You look very serious."

As serious as a heart attack.

He took a step forward, then another. He reached her, took the wine glass out of her hand, and set it on the counter. He cupped her cheeks, caressed her soft skin, and looked into her gaze. "Marry me."

Her dark eyes widened and her smile fell off her face. "Are you insane?"

Not the answer he would have hoped for, but he realized he had made a demand more than he had actually proposed to her. He had just seen her, and known this was his future. What he wanted, hell, what he needed to do.

He shook his head. "Not insane. Just very much into you. I've fallen in love with you and I want to be with you. For the rest of our lives."

She blinked. Her voice trembled. "You can't mean that... you don't even know me."

Brandon dropped his hands so he could take hers into his. His squeezed her hands gently. "I know everything I need to know. You're smart, kind, fierce, loving. You're stubborn and you're competitive as fuck. You're the best mother I could have ever asked for for Fallon. Someday, in the not totally distant future, when we've sorted all of this out, I want to make Fallon with you all over again." He kissed her softly. "We were meant to be."

Grace said, "I don't know what to say."

"Say yes." That seemed like an obvious response to him.

She nodded, like she was in agreement. Like she wanted to say yes. But her words showed hesitation. "What if you get bored?" she asked. "What if this whole playing happy family thing isn't really what you want? I can't do that to Fallon. I can't do that to me."

He was a little insulted, he wasn't going to lie, but he knew Grace was afraid. She was afraid to make the wrong decision and wind up alone raising a child the way she had before. He got that. But he wasn't going to stand there and argue with her. All he could do was prove himself to her and if that took time, it would take time. He was in for the long haul.

Right now, he was going to remind her of the chemistry between them.

Instead of answering her question he just dropped her hands, bent over, and scooped her up into his arms. She gasped in surprise but didn't protest. He settled her against his chest and marched down the hallway, toeing open the door to the room she was staying in. He set her down on the bed without a word and took her mouth with a hot, demanding, burning kiss. He needed her to understand he was telling the truth.

Grace wrapped her hands around his neck and kissed him back passionately, opening for him so that they were entwining tongues, taking and giving, intimately saying what they couldn't with words.

There was no going slow this time. He wanted her. All of her.

As usual, Grace was wearing shorts and a tank top. It seemed to be her summer uniform. It made it easy to strip her down. A couple of tugs and her shorts were off. He took her panties with them, not wanting to waste any time. He went straight for her pussy, laving his tongue over her.

She moaned, then bit her lip, as if she'd remembered Fallon was in the next room.

He ate her with a hard, driving passion, wanting everything he could milk from her. Grace was writhing, her hips rising to meet his strokes, and she was biting her hand to keep from screaming. It was the hottest thing he'd ever experienced.

She was about to explode. He could feel her thighs quivering, and her muscles tensing.

He pulled away from her fast and she gave a cry of disappointment.

"Why did you stop?" She was reaching for him, her eyes glazed, nipples hard beneath the cotton of her tank top.

"Let me inside you," he said. "If you say no, I will respect that and I'll give you the best orgasm of your life with my tongue. But if you say yes, I'm going to fuck you until you forget everything but the feel of my cock inside you."

He had a condom in his wallet and he reached into his pocket and pulled it out. Then he shucked his shirt and his shorts off while he gave her a chance to think about what she wanted. He knew she was on the pill. He'd seen her taking it, seen the pack lying on the bathroom counter in her toiletries bag. But he'd wear a condom to give her peace of mind.

When he turned back to her, he could see what her answer was going to be.

She had jumped off the cliff with him.

"I love you too," she said.

He hadn't expected it to hit him the way it did. It felt like a semi-truck barreling into him, knocking all the air out of his lungs briefly. Then he felt the most intense satisfaction and happiness he'd ever experienced. He wanted her so goddamn bad.

"Yeah?" he asked. "That makes me really fucking happy, Grace. You don't even understand."

"My answer is yes. Yes, I will marry you. Yes, you can fuck me."

When he looked down at her, tearing open the condom packet, he felt like he'd won the lottery. He didn't deserve her and she was afraid he wasn't man enough to stick around for the long haul, but he was going to spend every day proving that wasn't the case.

"You won't regret it, I promise."

SHE'D DONE IT AGAIN. She'd gotten lost in Brandon's blue eyes and given in to him.

But she couldn't help it. He'd asked her to *marry* him. He'd said he loved her.

She might be practical as hell but she was still a woman.

She wanted him inside her. She wanted him to love her. She wanted the fairy tale, nine years after the fact.

When he teased his tongue over her clit again, she forgot she was supposed to be quiet. She let out a sharp exhalation of air and encouraged him. "Yes, more. Please."

"More? You want more?" He shifted away.

Before she could protest he had the tip of his erection at her wet opening and he pushed inside her with one hard thrust.

Oh, wow. She closed her eyes, wanting to savor the moment. He felt like he was throbbing inside her. It was pure ecstasy.

Then he started to move and it was pure sweet torture. He started slow, but picked up speed rapidly, thrusting deep and hard inside of her. She held his arms, trying to be quiet in the dark room. An orgasm was building and she clung to him, wanting to explode, but not too soon.

Brandon seemed to know what she needed. He pulled out without warning. She gave a cry before she slapped her hand over her mouth to muffle the sound. She was going to ask what the hell he was doing when he went down on her again.

She was wet and aching and his tongue was doing amazing things to her. He teased at her clit, moved down her slit, pushed inside, until she was tensing again, heading toward release.

He moved his mouth away from her.

She couldn't believe it. He clearly wanted to draw this out too but damn...

Whatever she might have said got lost when he took her pussy again, his hips moving slowly this time, taking his time with her. Brandon wrapped his fingers in her hair and stared into her eyes.

"Grace. You feel perfect."

"So do you," she breathed, arching her hips to meet his thrusts.

But then he abandoned her again.

"Please," she whispered, spiraling in pleasure, and not even sure what she meant or needed. "Give it to me."

"What do you want, baby? My tongue? My cock?"

"Both."

He laughed softly and flicked his tongue over her clit. Then pull back.

"Damn it, Brandon," she cried. "Let me come."

His answer was to push inside her with his hard cock.

She had an orgasm immediately, closing her eyes and groaning through the waves of pleasure. Brandon pounded her with a fast, driving rhythm and she held onto him for dear life, lost in a haze of wet, aching passion.

It was intimate and powerful and bone-deep satisfying.

When he paused and then exploded inside her with gritted teeth, his fingers tightening in her hair. The moment lingered, then finally he relaxed, swallowing hard.

"Baby," he murmured. "Grace."

She stared up at him, overwhelmed in the best way possible. "Have we met before?" she said, giving him a grin.

Brandon laughed softly. "Yes. But I guess it wasn't our time. Now it is."

Grace was sticky and satisfied but that didn't prevent her from being stubborn. "Because you gave me the wrong number." She wasn't angry about it at this point, it was what it was. But that didn't mean she was going to let him pretend that fate had ripped them apart.

"My cock is still inside you and you want to argue about the phone number thing?" Brandon kissed her. "I swear I gave you my right number. It's the number I still have now. I've had the same cell number since I was fifteen."

He seemed earnest about the whole thing. Grace started to doubt herself. She still had the scrap of paper he'd written on. She had been carrying it in her wallet for nine years. It was jammed in between the discount card for the drugstore and her health insurance card. "Hang on. I have the paper."

Brandon shifted so he pulled out of her, but he seemed intent on starting something again. He was lazily stroking her nipple.

"Let me up." She pushed on his chest.

"Right now? Why?"

"I told you, I have the note you left me."

"You have it with you?" He looked stunned. What he didn't look was worried.

Which worried *her*. What the hell was going on with that note?

She climbed out of bed and padded across the room naked. She didn't have a traditional purse but a backpack purse that contained her wallet. She unzipped the wallet and fished out the little scrap of paper, now just a little yellow around the edge with age, and wrinkled.

The handwriting was sloppy. She took it over to the bed, where Brandon had flicked the bedside lamp on. He was rubbing his jaw. "What stupid thing did I write? I don't even remember. I just remember being rushed, Axl banging on the door telling me they would leave without me. My head was pounding and you were sleeping. I ripped the paper off of the notebook on your desk."

"It just says 'text me.'"

"Text me?" Brandon reached for the note. "That's so mid two thousands. And douchey."

Grace handed him the paper. "You did add three x's. But no name. I guess there was no way to sign it Brandon at that point."

"I don't recall the plan, but apparently, I was going to confess at some point. After you texted me, which you didn't." He looked at the note. "Grace, this is my number. I am not even kidding. Look at your phone. Hell, look at my phone. This is my number."

"That's impossible!" She was on her knees, very much naked, heart rate kicking into overdrive. She reached for her phone and found the number she'd had for Brandon for over a week now. Then she said, "Show me the note."

He did, holding it up.

She squinted and compared. "No, see, it's off by one number. That's a seven and you have a one written down."

"That's a seven written by a guy hungover as fuck and in a hurry."

Well, shit. She could see it now. But she'd been so upset when a girl had answered her text to the wrong number and then when Siobhan had told her Jeff Spicoli was the world's dumbest alias, she hadn't exactly tried multiple combinations or gotten a range of opinions. She had been humiliated, hurt, and pissed.

"Oh. My bad."

Brandon raised his eyebrows. "That's it? Nine years of thinking I'm a dickwad and that's all you have to say?"

Pretty much. "Whoops." She felt like an idiot all over again. "I'm sorry. I was just so embarrassed when I realized you gave me a fake name that I didn't have a very rational approach."

So... if she had stopped and tried different combinations she would have been able to tell him about Fallon before she was born? That was a shitty realization.

Brandon took the note from her and set it on the nightstand, along with her phone. "Grace. We both made mistakes. I was the idiot who gave you the fake name and I was the idiot who didn't attempt to contact you again. I could have found you on social media. But I was young and stupid and lazy. You were hurt and angry and thought you had the wrong number. There is nothing we can do about any of that now."

"But..."

He reached for her and pulled her into his arms. "But what? You would have told me you were pregnant? Probably. Who knows how that would have gone? I can't sit here and say I would have been a hands-on father at twenty-one. Maybe we would have wound up not liking each other."

She felt like he was just saying that to make her feel better but she could imagine that alternative reality too. She'd been young and spinning a fairy-tale future. Reality most likely would not have measured up to that expectation she had.

"You're right. It is what it is."

Brandon placed his hands on both of her ass cheeks and hauled her up against him. "Right now, it's pretty damn good."

It was. "Let's get in the hot tub."

"I thought you'd never ask."

THIRTEEN

GRACE HADN'T KEPT a secret this huge since she'd been pregnant with Fallon and terrified to tell her grandmother. But she knew the right thing to do was to ease Fallon into the idea of her and Brandon being together. Not just blurt out that they were getting married.

They had too many details to iron out first before they told her. Like where they were going to live. Or when they were actually going to get married. If they were going to have another baby any time soon.

None of those had been things they had talked about in the last two days in Beaver Bend. They had just stolen kisses when Fallon wasn't looking during the day, and a whole lot more at night.

It had been so much easier to just be in love in a house in the woods than to deal with reality.

Which was now on top of them as Brandon helped her take her suitcase up the stairs to her apartment. She had actually let him carry it, which he had teased her about. Fallon was running ahead. Grace's stomach was churning and she wasn't sure why. Part of her was defiantly proud of this tiny apartment. Part of her was embarrassed because it wasn't much.

But Brandon didn't look anything other than happy as they went inside. He was planning to spend the night, on the couch in case Fallon wandered into the living room, and then leave for Chicago in the morning.

"Want to see my room?" Fallon asked.

"Absolutely."

Fallon gave him a tour that made Grace feel like she might be watching too much HGTV with her daughter around. "Our style is farmhouse," Fallon told Brandon as she led him through the living room. "It's all about texture, not color."

Brandon shot Grace an amused look over his shoulder. "I see that. I like it."

Grace put her suitcase in her bedroom while Fallon showed Brandon her various treasures and the leaf presses they had hung on her walls. Fallon wasn't into bold and bright colors any more than she was. Her room was all ivories and greens.

"Want to see Mom's room?"

"Absolutely."

It's a good thing Grace and Brandon had crossed a line and they were having sex or this little tour would be a bit awkward. It was far too personal for the ancient baby daddy you wanted to keep at arm's length.

Even as it stood, it was awkward because she wanted nothing more than to shout out loud that she had a fiancé. She wanted Brandon to be spending the night with her in her bed. It was starting to bug her that she had yet to wake up next to him. Not nine years ago and not this week.

After years of lonely nights in this bed solo after long days exhausted from everything she had to do, Grace wanted to flip the narrative on her sad little bedroom.

"Very nice," Brandon said, eyeing her crowded room.

"Though you have a lot of stuff in here, Grace. How do you get in bed?"

"From the bottom." Her bed was against the window wall and she had crammed in her desk on the other side. It had only fit by her permanently leaving her closet door open so that her clothing and her desktop mingled together. Not ideal, but it worked. "I just kind of dive in."

"You are athletic, so I'm sure it works for you." He winked at her.

She was going to show him athletic in a few hours.

"Show him, Mom. Jump in bed."

"Fallon." She gave her daughter a look of reprimand. "Stop."

"Do it, do it!"

"Yeah, do it," Brandon said.

Since she had already captured the market on impulsive this week, what was one more silly move? "Fine. Back it up, give me room." She stepped back into the doorway and jogged the three steps and leaped onto her bed, Superman style.

Given that it wasn't the usual way she got into bed, she didn't know what she was doing. She went in hot, with too much air time, and she landed with a huge thump. "Oof, ow," she said, laughing.

She was midway through rolling over when Fallon jumped on her, knocking into her hip with her elbow. "Fallon!"

Her daughter was giggling and making a snow angel out of her bedsheets.

"Incoming."

Brandon raised his arms like he was going to jump on the bed too.

"No," Grace told him. "Absolutely not. Do not jump on this bed."

He ignored her and flung himself in their direction.

"Oh my God," Grace said, holding her arm up to block the

impact. He landed directly on her, flattening her beneath his muscular body.

It didn't hurt. It was just a whole lot of man on top of her and she couldn't do a damn thing about it.

"Hi," he said.

"Hi." If she wasn't mistaken a certain part of his anatomy was growing against her thigh. "You need to get off of me," she said softly, even as she wanted nothing more than to lie there with him forever.

"Spoilsport." He rolled over and grabbed Fallon and tickled her.

Grace was so overwhelmed by the unexpected domestic scene that she had to climb over the two of them and head into her living room. Not that it was any bigger but at least she wasn't crowded by her daughter and the man she had unexpectedly and randomly fallen in love with.

"You okay?" Brandon asked a minute or two later when he followed her into the living room.

She went over to her thermostat. "It's hot as hell in here."

"It's stuffy from being empty. Open a window." Brandon went over to the window and tried to open it.

"They're painted shut."

"You can't open the windows? I don't think that's safe." He frowned and ran his finger along the frame.

"It's fine," she said, flatly. She was sensitive about what she could afford. She knew that. She didn't think he was judging her, but at the same time she was defensive, she knew that.

Grace abandoned Brandon in the living room and went to Fallon's room to help her unpack. "We need to do all your laundry. Take everything out of your suitcase and put it in your laundry bag so we can take it downstairs."

"Can I help?" Brandon asked, standing in the doorway, hands in his pockets.

She looked at him, all casual sexiness, and her heart felt so damn full. "No. I'm good. Really good."

AFTER FALLON WENT TO BED, Grace turned on the TV so they could talk without Fallon hearing what they were saying. Brandon would have been content just to stare at Grace all night, amazed she'd said yes to him, but she wanted to iron out details. That was Grace. Efficient.

"What exactly do you do for a living?" she asked as they sat on her couch together. "I have vague notions about you buying and selling property, but I'm not entirely sure. I should probably know that."

"That's what I do. I buy shit no one wants and I make it shit someone wants." He brushed her hair off of her shoulder. He couldn't stop touching her. It was ridiculous. "The official term is investor."

He didn't care about work. He didn't want to talk about work. He wanted to talk about how soon he could get her naked. But Grace seemed nervous. He got the impression she didn't like him in her space. Maybe that she was afraid to tell Fallon about their relationship. Or worse, that she was having doubts about what they were doing.

"Like how many properties do you currently own?"

"Would you like me to send you my list of assets and my stock portfolio?" he asked, amused.

"What? No." Grace hit him in the chest with the palm of her hand. "I'm trying to figure out your life. We have all these things to figure out and talk about. Number one being where are we going to live?"

"Not here. I'm not as agile as you. I can't jump into bed every night."

She rolled her eyes. "I still have two months on my lease.

But I was thinking, even before you asked me to marry you, that I might want to move to Beaver Bend."

That caught him completely off guard. "What? Why?"

"Because it's clean, safe small-town living. Because people care about people there and Fallon has your parents there, not to mention fresh air and a yard to play in. She loves being outside."

"We can have a yard here in Minneapolis. My commute from here to Chicago would be no big deal. If you're living in Beaver Bend, when am I supposed to see you?"

She stared at him. "You can't move to Beaver Bend?"

"No, of course not. My business is in Chicago. I can't even move here right now, but I can get here every week, no problem." He could see that she was dismayed but given that they had just been discussing his business, he wasn't sure why she seemed so put out.

"Oh. I see. Well. You don't want us to move to Chicago?"

He hadn't really thought that was an option. "You could, but Fallon would have a lot of disruption that way. I'd have to sell my condo. We'd probably have to live out in the suburbs and I'm not sure that's totally what I want." He would love to stay downtown or get a brownstone in Lincoln Park, but that was not what he thought Grace had in mind for Fallon. "I thought you'd be concerned about too much change for Fallon."

Grace bit her lip and looked worried. "So, you want us to stay here and you stay in Chicago? Just to be clear."

Now he was a little concerned. Her tone was one of annoyance.

"That's not what I said. I'm not telling you it has to be that way forever. I'm just saying that I can't just up and leave my business tomorrow."

She nodded. "Okay. I understand. So why don't I just stay

here until my lease is up and we can think about it and look around for houses and stuff?"

"Perfect." Brandon was relieved. That had felt like it could go somewhere really dangerous very quickly. "We'll buy a house. Now kiss me."

"Fine. But no sex."

Brandon grinned at her. "I've heard that one before."

Grace rolled her eyes but she snuck him into her bedroom like she had all those years ago.

FOURTEEN

"YOU KNOW I think you're crazy," Siobhan said to her as she drove them both to the first house Grace was viewing.

"I know. I'm well aware of that fact. You've said it just about every day for a month since I got back from Beaver Bend." Grace looked around the window, eyeing the neighborhood with dismay. This was the third house today Brandon had scheduled for her to see and each one was bigger and more pretentious than the last. "This neighborhood is so not me. I feel like everyone is going to think I'm someone's nanny."

"More likely they're going to assume your fiancé is like fifty-five. You're going to be a trophy wife, how sweet is that?"

Grace was already feeling weird about shopping for houses, that he would be buying, without Brandon. The price range was higher than she thought was necessary or appropriate. She hadn't even realized he was thinking in these enormous and expensive terms until he'd sent her the addresses she was meeting the real estate agent at. She was supposed to be prescreening and narrowing it down to one or two. So far, she'd seen a new build that looked like an enormous white box on a postage stamp lot, and an eighties disaster that needed all new everything. There was no way she felt comfortable taking on a renovation. She hadn't ever even expected to buy a house, let alone remodel one. It was too overwhelming.

This was a pretty neighborhood with big trees and beautiful homes and she felt way out of her element.

Siobhan was not helping.

"Being a trophy wife is not a label I ever want," she told her friend.

"Where is Brandon, by the way?"

"He had a business trip to New York. He'll be back in Chicago on Thursday, but he won't be here until Friday."

"I can't believe you're marrying Jeff Spicoli." Siobhan shook her head. "I didn't see that one coming."

That made her laugh. "Me either."

"I think it's this one." Siobhan pulled into a driveway with a side-entry garage.

The agent was already on the front walkway. "Isn't this gorgeous?" she said.

"Yes, it's beautiful." The agent, Gloria, reminded Grace of Susan, Brandon's mother. Put together, polished, confident.

Grace shoved her phone in her back pocket, wishing she had thought to bring a purse. She needed something to do with her hands.

They went in through the front door into a soaring two-story entryway. Beyond that was an open concept family room and gourmet kitchen.

"We'll take it," Siobhan said.

Grace rolled her eyes. The agent laughed.

"The hardwood floors have just been refinished. The kitchen has a six-burner stove and quartz countertops. There is a walk-in pantry and everything is wireless. You can turn your heat up or down remotely on your phone or tablet, turn on your oven, look inside your refrigerator while you're at the grocery store."

"That's impressive," Grace said, even as she knew there was no way in hell she could live in this house. If they bought this house, she would feel like the world's crappiest trophy wife. One who had none of her own money *and* sucked at looking pretty.

There was no way she could visualize herself in this house with Fallon and Brandon, especially if he was only with them thirty percent of the time. She'd rather get a townhome or move to Beaver Bend. Neither of which Brandon was on board with. He was convinced they needed a house to grow in to, whatever that meant.

She couldn't rattle around a huge house with one child all by herself. It just wasn't her vibe. She was used to being in a very small space and while crowded and frequently annoying, there was something cozy about it. She wanted a medium house, not a mega house.

"Let's head upstairs."

Grace couldn't do it. "Gloria, I'm sorry, this isn't the house for me. I think we should just cancel the rest of the houses this afternoon. I don't think we're going in the right direction and I don't want to waste your time."

"What?" Gloria looked alarmed. "We can cancel the houses scheduled if you'd like, but let me know where we're going wrong here and I can steer us in the right direction. Brandon seemed very excited about these houses."

Grace blew out her breath. "You did exactly what Brandon asked for, trust me. I think he and I need to decide together what our vision is and then we'll get back to you." Because if they moved in to a place like this she would feel like a stranger in another woman's house.

Without waiting for a response, she fast-walked out of the

gorgeous house and to Siobhan's car. She had a text from Brandon.

Any contenders?

No.

Siobhan got in the car and slammed the door shut behind her. "What the hell was that? That poor Gloria chick thinks you're firing her. She's seeing her January vacation to Punta Cana disappear before her eyes."

"That's not the kind of house I want."

Grace could feel her friend staring at her but she refused to look up from her phone screen resting in her lap.

"What kind of house do you want?"

"Not that one."

"That clears it up." Siobhan started the car. "I think you're having control issues. You're used to running the show and now Brandon is in your life and you have to discuss before you do."

Grace felt her jaw drop. "What show was I running? The shit show? I was surviving, not making decisions."

"Think about it. This is a huge change for you. You're used to being tough, not someone's kept woman."

"Brandon is not treating me like a kept woman. We're partners." They were. She didn't doubt that for a minute.

So, that did lead to the question, what was her problem? It was a valid concern and Siobhan's accusation unnerved her.

"Hold on. Liam is calling me."

"Sullivan and Sloane's dad?" Grace asked, startled.

"Yes." She answered the call. "Hey, hottie. How are you? I miss you."

Okay. That did not sound like a woman who hadn't spoken to a hookup since she'd rolled out of his bed in the morning. Siobhan had clearly been keeping secrets.

Feeling like an idiot sitting there listening to Siobhan's very flirtatious conversation, she called Brandon. "Hey. I'm sorry, I'm not feeling these houses. I want something smaller."

"Smaller? Are you serious?"

"Yes. I feel weird in these huge houses. Especially since I'm going to be alone there half the time." She sounded like a brat, which she despised. "I'm just used to being able to see everything all at once. And I can't have a wooded lot. Where do you think serial killers emerge from?"

Brandon laughed. "Grace. There are no serial killers in the suburbs. They stick to the city or the country, but never a subdivision."

"See, that's just so wrong. There are killers everywhere, and that's how they fool you. You let your guard down then wham. Lawyer serial killer living right next door."

"Pick whatever house you want, baby. I'm fine with whatever. But we should try to close on something as soon as possible. Preferably before I leave for Asia in three weeks. Otherwise we'll have to hire the movers to move you out of the apartment, then store your stuff, then move it again."

That sounded about as fine as a root canal. "When do you get back?"

"January seventh."

Grace almost dropped her phone. Siobhan was giggling and saying something about a blowjob. So clearly, she had heard Brandon wrong. "What? Say that again?"

"January seventh. Remember, I told you it was a longer trip. I was planning on six months but I scaled it back to four."

What. The. Fuck. "You said a longer trip. I thought that meant like two weeks. You never said four fucking months. Brandon, you're going to miss Fallon's birthday! Thanksgiving! Christmas! New Year's Eve, oh my God."

She felt like she was going to throw up. She was so angry her eyes filled with hot, raging tears.

They hadn't told Fallon they were together yet but of course she was going to assume he would be around for her birthday and the holiday season. Why wouldn't she? Grace sure in the hell had.

"I'm sorry, baby, it's just bad timing. I couldn't shift anything around. After this, I'll make sure it doesn't conflict with family time."

"I knew you would do this," she choked out, through hot tears. "No compromise. We're supposed to fit into your life, not the other way around."

"Calm down. It's just a miscommunication."

"Like when you told me your name was Jeff Spicoli."

It was a low blow and she knew it.

"That's not cool," Brandon said. "Is that going to be thrown in my face every time you're upset?"

Maybe.

"I have a right to be upset."

"So do I. You basically just said you knew I would let you down." Brandon swore. "Grace, I have to go. My flight is boarding."

"Fine. Goodbye." She was so furious she hung up without waiting for his reply or telling him she loved him.

Siobhan was staring at her wide-eyed. "Is everything okay?"

"No." Stinging tears just poured down her cheeks without warning and she felt like her heart was breaking. "I think I just broke up with Brandon."

"Oh, sweetie, you don't want to do that. You're just scared. You're used to being the tough guy. It's hard to be vulnerable with someone."

She swiped at her face and turned to her friend. "He forgot to mention that he's going to Asia for four months. He's missing Fallon's birthday, Thanksgiving, Christmas... this would be his first birthday with her."

Siobhan's jaw dropped. "Fucking dump his ass. After you kick it. Final answer."

"I did. I will." But it was the most devastating feeling. She'd been worried about this and here it was. He wouldn't live with them, he wouldn't give up an extended trip, he didn't want to come out to his friends or family.

She sucked at keeping secrets and she sucked at being anything other than stubbornly independent.

"He's calling me," she said, throwing her phone at Siobhan like it was on fire. "I'm scared if I answer it, I'll give into him. And I'll get pregnant and that will be that."

"Sweetie, you can't get pregnant over the phone. I've tried." But Siobhan took her phone and stuck it in her bra. "I've got your back. Call your brother to take Fallon tonight. We're having a wine night at my house."

GRACE WASN'T ANSWERING his calls.

They were doing priority boarding. He was flying business class, but he still had time. They had thirty rows to board before they closed the door.

He called Rick, because he trusted him to be rational. "I could have sworn I told Grace I was going to be gone for four months," he told him, pacing in his business suit by the newsstand.

"Did she freak out when you told her that?"

"No."

"Then you did not fucking tell her you were going to be gone four months, dude. No one in a new relationship is going to be cool with that. There would have been questions, concerns. Did any of that happen?"

"No." Damn it. Maybe, if he were honest, he'd been afraid to tell her. For this very reason. "I think she broke up with me.

She told me I am not compromising." He adjusted his tie, and set his computer bag down on an empty seat by the gate. "I'm compromising. I'm buying a house in Minneapolis. Isn't that compromise?"

"But you're not moving there."

"No. I can't."

"Did she refuse to move to Chicago to be with you?"

"No."

"Dude."

"What?"

"Think about what you just said."

Oh. "She thinks I'm going to keep my old life and have her too."

"Give the guy a gold star."

"She might not think I'm going to cheat on her, but she feels like a side note."

"Right again. Let her move to Chicago if she wants to. Seriously. Show her she's a priority." There was a rustling sound and Rick lowered his voice, like he didn't want Sloane to hear him. "You think I wanted to buy Sloane's childhood house? No. I don't like mowing grass. I'd rather be riding my bike. But it's what she wants, so I bought a ride-on mower. Let Grace live wherever she wants."

Brandon felt like he had heartburn. He'd drunk too much coffee and then he had been a giant dumbass. "So, what do I do now?"

"Go get her and drive her back to Chicago, without the kid, and talk to her. Have sex. Buy real estate."

"I'm at O'Hare. I'm about to fly to New York."

"You get on that plane, enjoy the bachelor life because that's what you will be living."

He knew Rick was right. "Fuck." He stared at everyone

boarding and tried to calculate how pissed off his colleagues would be if he missed this meeting.

Then he realized it didn't matter.

Grace mattered.

GRACE OPENED the door to her apartment, expecting her brother.

It was Brandon, wearing a suit and an expression of contrition.

"Baby."

"What are you doing?" she asked, even as she felt tears rise. Dang it, she was not a crier. Why was he making her so emotional? "I thought you were going to New York today."

He took a step forward. Instinctively, she took a step back.

"I was at the gate, as they called my boarding group, and my fiancée, the woman I love, hung up on me. So here I am."

"I didn't hang up on you," she said, because that mattered for no reason other than she was stubborn.

"I'm sorry I upset you. I shouldn't have been so casual about something that is a big deal." He stepped in and closed the door behind him. "This is a deal I've been brokering for a year and I was so focused on making it work, I didn't adjust to this new reality."

"What new reality?" she asked, wanting him to spell it out.

"This." He pointed between them. "You. Me. Fallon."

"I haven't either. I think I'm struggling to give up control. I'm used to calling the shots."

"We both are. So how about we stop trying to steal the puck from each other and come up with a game plan instead?"

Grace nodded, ridiculously relieved. For the last three hours, she had been convinced she'd tossed out the best thing to ever happen to her as impulsively as she'd stumbled into it.

"I can do that," she whispered.

"We can live in Chicago if you want. And I'll rework the trip to Asia to three separate trips, two weeks each, but I won't miss any major life events. Is that fair?"

"Yes."

"And I'm buying that house in Beaver Bend so we can spend summers there. That is, if you want to."

She nodded again, choked up. "I'm sorry I called you Jeff Spicoli." She was. She wanted to look forward, not backward. She reached out and touched his tie. "You look very handsome in a suit."

"You look amazing naked."

That made her laugh. "How romantic."

Brandon cupped her cheeks, and gave her a soft kiss. "I love you."

"I love you, too." She did, with everything in her stubborn heart. "Fallon is going to Juan's tonight. In twenty minutes, you can bust out a purple party condom."

"I like that game plan."

EPILOGUE

BRANDON STOOD AT THE ALTAR, ready to seal the biggest deal of his life. His father was standing next to him and he leaned in and murmured, "Don't screw this up, kid. She's the best thing to happen to you."

He gave his father an amused look. "That's your wedding day advice? Don't screw it up."

"That's all I've got. Make it count."

"I plan on it." Brandon shook his father's hand, who took a seat next to Brandon's mother. He glanced down at his groomsmen, his best friends since childhood. They were all smiling, except for Sullivan.

Rick gave him an exaggerated thumbs-up.

They had all cleaned up pretty well.

They were getting married in his parents' church. It was an old stone building, set back from the road. It was a perfect winter day, with blue, sunny skies, and a pristine white snowfall blanketed everything from an overnight dusting.

When the bridesmaids came down the aisle, he barely saw them. Grace had insisted Juan be on the bride's side of the wedding party, and he looked uncomfortable with that fact, going first down the aisle in his suit that matched the groomsmen. Brandon got her point. Juan was standing up for her, not for him, even though they had been getting along great since the engagement. Grace wasn't about tradition, she was about heart, and he was cool with that. Her sister-in-law was a bridesmaid, along with Siobhan and Leighton, who had become fast friends with Grace.

Fallon was the maid of honor. When she came down the aisle, Brandon felt his vision blur from tears. She was wearing a butter yellow dress that made her look older than she was. Her curls had been tamed, and she was very solemn as she walked toward the front of the church. He couldn't imagine his life without her in it now. What the hell had he been doing before Grace told him he had a daughter? Nothing that seemed particularly important now in comparison.

Five months and Fallon had stolen his heart entirely.

When she got to the front he gave her a wink.

She giggled.

He and Grace were prepared for hard questions and some angst in the teen years about why they hadn't been together most of her early life, but for now, she just seemed happy that her parents were together.

Then Grace stepped through the doorway and Brandon forgot how to breathe.

She had chosen a form-fitting dress and no veil. Just loose caramel waves tumbling around her face. Her body was long and lean and her chest was pushing up with a hint of cleavage. He took all that in with one sweep of his eyes. But what really got him was the smile on her face. She was beaming. She looked gorgeous and in love. With him.

He wasn't worthy.

But he was going to take his father's advice and not screw this up.

"Hi," she said when she reached him, eyes sparkling.

"Hi." Then because he didn't need to cater to tradition either, he bent down and kissed her. Her mouth was just too tempting.

"You're jumping the gun there, but I applaud enthusiasm," the minister said.

Everyone laughed.

Brandon didn't hear the majority of the ceremony. It was a blur of words and movements. He only had eyes and ears for Grace. The moment she said "I do," he didn't think he could be any happier.

When the minister said, "I'm pleased to introduce you to Mr. and Mrs. Brandon and Grace Blackwell," the room erupted in cheers and clapping.

Fallon leaped out of her seat and said, "Huzzah!"

That made him laugh. Where did she get this stuff from?

"Come here, kiddo," he said. "Walk down the aisle with me and Mom."

Grace reached for Fallon's hand and they exited the church, together.

GRACE WAS PROBABLY the happiest she had ever been in her entire life. She was married. To the father of her daughter. It was crazy and full circle and everything she could have ever imagined.

The dance floor at their reception was chaotic, silly, and full of all the people she loved the most in the world.

Thanks to Leighton, they'd pulled this wedding off in record time, which was good, because life had been crazy. They had moved to Chicago, to a very cool brownstone in Bucktown with a price tag that had nearly made her heart stop, but Brandon thought was a sound investment. They had also bought the house in the woods in Beaver Bend, which was where they were staying this week.

And she'd just found out she was pregnant.

"Having fun?" Brandon asked her, giving her a kiss on the top of her head.

"Yes. Look at Fallon." Their daughter was line dancing with zero rhythm. She and Jesse were side by side, both awkward as hell but clearly having fun.

"She didn't get her moves from us, that's for sure."

Grace laughed. "Nope." She fanned herself. "It's hot in here." It was the pregnancy. She'd been having random hot flashes for a week now.

"Come outside with me for a minute." He took her hand and led her to the patio doors.

The reception was at a small venue in the woods, with a whole glass wall overlooking the woods. The doors led to an extensive deck that would be beautiful in the summer but now was covered under a blanket of snow.

"It's snowing," she said as he opened the door for her. "It's so beautiful."

"It's like the night we met." Brandon led her into the middle of the deck. "Dance with me."

Grace threw her head back and stared up at the stars in the sky. The snow gently drifted down, landing on her eyelashes. It was the night they met. She righted her head and stared into her husband's eyes. He pulled her against him and they started to sway.

"I need to have a talk with your lawyer," she said.

Brandon frowned. "What? Why?"

"Because you told me he would put it in writing that you wouldn't get me pregnant and he was clearly slacking on the job. No paperwork. And guess what?" She grinned up at him.

For a second his face was blank, then his lips split into a smile. “Are you saying... are you pregnant?”

She nodded. “Yes, I am.” She had gone off the pill knowing they would want to try in about a year, but they had been using protection. They were two for two with condoms.

“But we use condoms.”

Grace raised her eyebrows. “And that’s clearly not working for us. Something to note moving forward from here.”

Brandon laughed. “Same kids, same sandbox. You were right.” He turned and cupped his hand over his mouth and yelled in the general direction of the reception. “Grace was right.”

That made her laugh. “Are you happy?”

He nodded. “Very. You aren’t going to sue me for breach of a verbal contract, are you?”

“Nope. I’ll even let you name this baby.”

“How about we do that together?”

“Deal.”

Brandon dipped her unexpectedly. Grace laughed, breathless.

The slider opened. “Hey, you two, save that for later.” It was Axl. “People want the cake cut. People like cake.”

Grace let her husband tug her by the hand and back into their reception.

“I am so glad you were stripping,” she told him. “Or I may have never found you.”

Brandon gave her a wink. “Wait until later.”

She couldn’t wait.

ABOUT THE AUTHOR

USA Today and New York Times Bestselling author Erin McCarthy sold her first book in 2002 and has since written over seventy novels and novellas in romance and mysteries. Erin has a special weakness for tattoos, high-heeled boots, Frank Sinatra, and dive bars. She lives with her husband and their blended family of kids and rescue dogs.

Connect with Erin:
www.erinmccarthy.net

ALSO BY ERIN MCCARTHY

Tap That Series

Stripped Down

Strip Search

Strip Tease

Strip Away (releases 2019)

Stripped Bare (releases 2019)

68450860R00112

Made in the USA
Columbia, SC
08 August 2019